a rising tide of people swept away

Scott Archer Jones

Fomite
Burlington, VT

ISBN-13: 978-1-942515-43-2
Library of Congress Control Number: 2015960523

Fomite
58 Peru Street
Burlington, VT 05401
www.fomitepress.com

This novel is dedicated to the working poor — those who labor fifty or sixty hours a week and still are a half step from ruin.

Acknowledgements

I acknowledge that this book is a mythic Albuquerque, but I believe New Mexicans will recognize the Valley's spirit.

I am much obliged to Antonya Nelson's class at the Taos Writers Conference, where this book first debuted as a short story. John Dufresne's master class fixed several stubborn issues in the novel. My editor Phaedra Greenwood as usual cut hundreds of extraneous adverbs as well as kept me honest. My wife Sandra Hornback Jones read and massaged each of the drafts and yet remains married to me.

CHAPTER ONE

Slap in the middle of the Albuquerque strip shopping center, Rip's Bar and Package Liquor dominated its accidental, sagging skyline. First of all, it stacked up a full two stories while other places squatted on the street as one-story nests of cinder block. Second, it had a 50's front made of narrow blonde stone, forming a planter and a wall that carried a ribbon window above chest height. The window ran black against the facade, but three beer signs glimmered through the glass dimly during the day and brightly at night. Rip's did not resemble the village center. It did resemble one of Albuquerque's lost souls.

Across the street a small boy came pounding around the corner of the Thrift Store. He was dressed in a torn T-shirt and shorts, dingy socks and cheap sneakers. With a huff he threw himself under the table out front of the Thrift. He scuttled back against the wall of the store, sucked himself into a ball, and tried to breathe slow, quiet. He could hear running footsteps. Staring sideways, back the way he came, he saw cargo shorts, tanned legs, two large expensive athletic shoes. They stopped right in front of him. Stuffed under the large flat deck of the table, he held his breath. His view of the legs cut off at the thighs. He saw the toes point right, then scuff around to the left. They faced across the street. With a gritty sound on the pavement, they came full around and pointed at him. He held his breath.

He heard the curse, "Chingado." One of the feet kicked a rock down the street. The shoes scuffed off. He waited as long as he could, and only then let out a long, ragged breath. He eased himself up to the front of the table, so he could scan up and down the street. He would wait here.

The strip smelled of trouble, filled with stores that wobbled on the edge of bankruptcy. It had always been in trouble though, and the locals reacted to their impending financial failures with fatalism that matched the overall seediness of the storefronts. First on the right crouched Cut 'n Curl, the hairdresser's, with a cheery window hung with pink shears and a regular house door freighted with sleigh bells. The awning overhead missed most of its edging and now sagged alarmingly. Across the way, the boy contemplated the heads that moved back and forth inside the Curl. He was dark, and as dusty as the straggly tree hanging over the street in front of him, a tree that erupted from a two-foot square of litter and cigarette butts. His gaze shifted to the left, to the next store.

Bob's Taxidermy leaned up shoulder to shoulder with Cut 'n Curl. Bob's glass had once been painted in child's tempura with an elk poised above a cliff and surrounded with dwarfish conifers. The paint had long since started dropping to the floor inside as dust, and the elk had developed a mange of transparency – Bob himself often stared out through the withers of the beast, waiting. The boy didn't like Bob, but he did like the elk.

The strip also owned a combination locksmith and Christian bookstore establishment, Key to the Kingdom, and a taco stand, Julio's Taquería. A pawnshop, Enchanted Valley Cash 4 U, squatted by a bail bondsman known as Soulful. Soulful had titled his place

AAA Slammer Relief and hung his windows with stout bars that showed the rusting permanence of an old state penitentiary. Irony ran up and down the street, laughingly dark under the New Mexico sun, but the boy didn't feel it. He felt hungry. Crawling out from under the table, the boy drew his arms back into the body of his oversized tee shirt, leaving the sleeves flapping, and wiggled his shoulders back and forth. He crossed the street, went down a narrow opening between the Bail Bond office and the pawnshop. Appearing armless, he ricocheted down the two walls to the dumpster at the back.

———

AT NINE A.M., RED DONNIE furtively approached Rip's door. He scratched at the aluminum handle set in tinted glass, much like a dog asking to be let in. In a moment the bolt clacked once and the door opened. The guardian of the entrance, a silver-haired man, stepped back so that Red Donnie could enter. Red Donnie eased inside, and the glass closed on its hydraulic piston. "Thank you, Tenn," he said.

"Sorry I'm late opening. We were up until about midnight. Susan was having another crisis, and the boys wanted to help her out." Tenn led the way, all five feet of him, and Red Donnie followed, towering over him by a foot and a half. The short man marched, shoulders back and head held high, while the tall man threw his feet out in front of him with a scuffing sound. Donnie, his hair tied back in a ponytail, bent forward, casting a shadow over his friend. Their trail was cloaked in dust motes limned by the window's harsh light. Tenn rounded the counter and stepped up, suddenly becoming six feet high. Red Donnie folded up, a stork on a barstool, and pecked his head forward out of his shoulders. They were eye to eye, the old and the middle-aged.

3

"Have you seen the boy this morning?" Red Donnie flinched as he asked and diverted his eyes obliquely away.

Tenn squinted up his left eye. "Wasn't out back when I hauled out the trash." The bartender set up a shot glass, filled it, and pulled a light beer.

While he waited, Red Donnie prodded a bar mat back and forth. "Listen, Tenn. We should do something. It's our Christian duty. Either that or our karmic need."

"Karmic need? That's a leftover from your hippie days?"

Red Donnie ducked his head like a youngster. "We're talking about the boy."

Tenn said, "What would you do, then? He's going to run wild. You know that."

"He's a good boy."

"Actually," said the bartender and paused. "Actually, you don't know that."

Red Donnie replied, "We're all innocent as children."

"I doubt he's been raised very innocent in that house."

"That's why he left, why he's always leaving. He turns his back on the things that happen there." The tall man slurped at his beer, and threw the shot into his mouth. The whiskey drew his face taut and he appeared older, closer to his fifty-eight years.

Tenn said, "You've never even talked to him, or at least he's never talked to you. Damn few people have heard him speak."

"He needs a good home."

"Well, Donnie, you sure can't give him one. Even if he let you, you couldn't take him home to your mother. If you don't mind me saying so, your mother is a terror."

Red Donnie raised up from the counter, dropped his elbows down at his sides. "Mother is a fine Christian woman. Sometimes

4

she can be sharp tongued." He dug in his pocket and produced four crumpled dollar bills and a quarter. "Time to go to work. Watch out for the boy, if just for me."

"I tell you what. I'll set some food out for him. You can owe me."

—⁓—

TENN WOULDN'T HAVE ANOTHER REAL customer for a couple of hours, so he had time. He slipped a paper plate out from beneath the counter, jerked a bag of potato chips off the rack, and added a plastic packet of two hygienically sealed jerky strips. From the bar refrigerator he hauled out a jug of two percent milk and filled a beer mug with it. He trod through the package liquor part of his establishment and into the back storeroom. There a scratched and battered door hung open on its uneven hinges, and Tenn could see through the screen door into the alley. He kicked the rickety screen open with his foot, and caught its edge on his knee as he stepped out. He stooped the short distance needed and set the plate and glass on the back step.

For the next hour, Tenn unloaded the dishwasher, swept the floor, and settled all the chairs back on the ground. He waited behind the counter, working Sudokus.

At ten, the paperboy arrived. The front door creaked and Tenn glanced up from the puzzle. "Hi there, Cabell."

A young man hesitated in Rip's door. He stuck his head further into the room, then back out into the street, turning first to the right and then left. "Have you seen the boy?"

"Which one?"

"The homeless one."

Tenn said, "He's not as homeless as some. He just doesn't go home."

"He sleeps outside and eats out of dumpsters."

"Everybody got to make their choices."

The young man shrugged.

Tenn hesitated, softened the judgment. "He's doing okay. You watching out for him now?"

"No. Curious, that's all. Here's your paper." He clumped across the floor in immense unlaced sports shoes and held out the folded *Albuquerque Journal*. "Why do you call me Cabell?"

"Your name is Calloway, isn't it?"

"Yes, but...." Calloway's voice died off. He shuffled his huge feet twice, and deposited his canvas bag on one of the stools.

Tenn said, "Cab Calloway was a singer. Look, your folks named you Ignatius, right?"

"Right."

"And you don't like that name, right?"

"No."

"So, get another one."

Calloway scratched behind his ear. "What other one?"

"If you won't pick...."

"What?"

"Then I will."

Calloway said, "I'll think about it. You always make things harder than they have to be."

"Sit down and I'll make you a limeade."

"Can't. The *Journal* comes out 365 days a year, and I gotta make my rounds."

"I'll make you one to go. Wait there and I'll be done in a jiff."

Calloway leaned on a barstool, dressed in shorts, a tee shirt and a jacket. His hair hung in bangs across his tanned forehead.

"Say, Cabell, aren't you hot in that jacket? It's not exactly winter."

"Might rain, later."

"Might not." Tenn slid a red plastic cup across to the paperboy.
"I worry he might get wet, if it rains."

"Who might get wet?"

"You know. GMR."

"The boy? He's got sense. He'll find a doorway or a shed and stay dry."

Unconvinced, Calloway turned to go, "Thanks, for the limeade."

———

REGINA TALMADGE KNELT IN HER bathroom and beheld her black skin, more lustrous than the white porcelain beneath her hands. All around a light rained down from the ceiling. The shadow of her head was dark, like a byzantine icon of a black Madonna and the hot, bare bulb above created a gloriole showering around the back of her head. She knelt there naked, her wide hips, her small breasts offered up. Staring at her round Madonna abdomen below her protruding curved ribs, she thought, Not enough, not enough. Still fat. She closed her eyes, unwilling to see this part. She gave a small, tentative heave, and it grew, the two breakfast burritos fountaining out into the catchment below her. Her abdominal muscles jerked - and her breath billowed out hoarsely in a huuhnh. Fumbling with her left hand Regina reached up and tripped the handle, listened to the cleansing rush of water and the final belching gurgle as it carried her weakness out and down, hidden. It was getting easier – she didn't have to use her index finger anymore. She levered herself up with a satisfied grunt, and reached for the breath mints on the back of her john.

———

AT ELEVEN FIFTEEN, THE SCREEN door in back opened, and Regina came through Rip's, her short heels clocking and her African butt swaying behind her. She claimed a table near the end of the counter. She carried a baked potato in a paper boat, with napkin and plastic fork clasped underneath. "Hey, Tenn. There's a beer mug full of flies on your back step."

He blew past her announcement. "The usual, Regina?" She nodded, and he proceeded to make a Rum and Diet Coke.

"The flies are on milk. Or in it. Why do you keep milk here anyway?"

"For Richard's White Russians."

"Why do you have milk on your back step?"

"The boy, Regina. He might eat lunch here, much as you do. Why *do* you eat your lunch here?"

"They play the TV in the Potato Barn. Besides, they don't serve Rum and Coke."

Tenn came around the counter and placed the drink down in front of her. He glanced at her neck and neckline, checking out her collarbone standing out from her shoulder like a flag. "You've lost some weight, Regina."

"You think so?" She smiled, a tiny grin. "You old liar." After that, she was silent for a bit as she ate, or at least she didn't talk. Regina did make cooing sounds as she shoved the fork into the potato, and umph'ing sounds as she moved her jaws around the food.

"Good potato?"

She said with her mouth full. "It's a potato, Tenn. It's only the butter and the sour cream and the jalapeños and cornichons that make it."

"I think I'll stick to my cheese sandwich." Tenn went back to his sentinel's place where he made a big show of wiping down the counter with a towel.

The glass door in front rattled. In warning, Tenn said, "It's time for Harry."

Sunlight suddenly spilled in, and a shout from the sidewalk echoed into Rip's. "We got the place surrounded. Come out with your hands up."

Regina shouted back, "Harold Llewellyn Weissman, you get your saggy fat ass in here, and stop terrorizing the neighborhood!"

Harry advanced two steps into Rip's and posed, each hand held out in the ta-da gesture. The door eased shut behind him. He flared his eyes in the muted light, wrinkling his tall forehead, and reached up, delicately touching his bald crown. He rubbed his hand through his goatee, and turned his eyes around in a considering fashion.

Tenn said, "Coming or going, Harry?"

"Well, you've twisted my arm. Lets hope you don't waste my whole afternoon drinking, like you did last week."

"I heard it was day before yesterday," said Regina.

"Naah, day before yesterday I was making deliveries for Bob the Taxidermy Guy. He's not stuffing many heads, but he's doing great dressing out game for people. Course, I don't think the Health Department has ever been in the back to check him out."

Tenn grinned. "So, you're driving all over Albuquerque in your dead-ass Japanese car delivering bootleg deer?"

"It's one of my business interests, yes. Besides, I delivered elk and turkey also." Harry advanced on Regina's table. He seized the chair opposite her, sinking his dusty suit and small frame down into it with a gingerly glide. He planted his phone on the table between them.

Regina played it up. She grimaced horribly at him, her lips flattening into a thin line. "Ain't no other tables you could sit at in here? Looks like a pretty empty bar to me." Regina waved her plastic fork around the place.

Harry leaned forward. "An educated woman like you, Regina,

saying 'ain't.' It's a mockery of all that college your Daddy paid for."

Regina leaned back away from Harry. "College never helped me any more than being a Jew has helped you. I bet the folks down at the Synagogue don't steer much business your way."

"Been a long time since I've been to Synagogue, Regina. I'm more of a citizen of the benign universe now." Harry leaned back to get Tenn into his view. "Could I have a beer then, barkeep? One of the kosher ones?"

"And which one would that be?"

"You know, comes out of a brass spigot underneath a big handle."

Tenn drew the beer, and set the tall glass in front of Harry. "There you are. Kosher as we got."

"Thanks then, Tenn. What's new?"

"UNM has lost again. The Council is getting more corruption accusations from the *Journal*. And the police were around to the house in back again last night."

"The crack house?"

"No, not that one, that's four blocks over. This is the one with the drunks."

"Oh," said Regina. "The boy's folks. Did you phone in the complaint?"

Tenn replied, "Bars don't normally complain about the neighbors – it's usually the other way around."

Harry asked, "What's the setup over there? Is it a cult or something? Is it drugs?"

"Don't think so. No dope smells, no unexplained thefts. I think it's only a party house full of binge drinkers. GMR's folks have what you would call friends over all the time. It's a wonder the kids ever get any sleep."

Regina asked, "Why do you call the boy G-M-R?"

"Don't know where it came from, but a lot of people call him GMR. His real name is Gerald Matthew Roger Whittington. He gave me the full name real serious, when he finally introduced himself."

Regina snorted, "He talked to you? He hasn't said a word to anyone else." Tenn gave her the eye.

Harry asked, "So the boy doesn't live with his party parents anymore?"

Regina supplied, "He ran away from home, a whole block. You see him around, and maybe he goes home sometimes, but who can tell?"

"So, how old is he? He appeared so short and scrawny, last time I saw him."

Regina said, "He's ten."

"Are you sure?" Tenn's forehead creased up between his eyes. "I thought maybe seven." Rip's door swung open and a party of four trooped in. He turned to scurry back behind his counter, up on his raised floor.

―――

BEDROOMS SHOULD BE DARK, SHELTERED, but this one was more. It had been filled with secrets, and secluded from the world. The sole inhabitant opened the laptop on the bed and lay down beside it. Inside, children posed foolishly like adults, naked, tiny penises centered by the lens. The boys gaped out big-eyed off the screen. A white hand reached gently to the photos, going from one to the next, caressed them, possessive. Breath sighed ragged in the glow of the screen.

SUMMER 2009

CHAPTER TWO

WEARING SHORTS, A TEE SHIRT, a plaid long sleeve, and beat-up tennis shoes, Gerald Matthew Roger Whittington crouched in the alley and poked a stick under a spider. The boy encouraged the bug to ramble its way onto the twig, where it lazily waved its front legs. When it climbed its way up close to his hand, he tossed the stick away and recoiled back. Some spiders bite.

GMR made his way up the alley to the back of a welding shop. Peering to the left and the right, skulking, he ducked through the open garage door, squatted down behind the shop's clutter, and listened for any sound of people. Satisfied by the silence, he crept into a restroom. When the boy finished, he opened the door of the bathroom, listened, flushed the toilet, and bolted out the door across the alley, where he wedged in behind a dumpster. The welding shop still stretched back away from him silent and still, so he crawled out from his hiding place. He scuffed his feet as he wandered away, stopped where a dust dune had collected by a light pole, and used the toe of his shoe to write his initials, GMR.

Mid-afternoon heat attacked his shoulders and neck, and he felt perspiration on his forehead. Moving out of the alley, the boy took to the sidewalk and headed towards the old village center. He stumped along as he went, hurried through the sunlit patches and lingered in the shade where dusty old cottonwoods provided deep carpets of darkness.

The building read "Alfredo Gonzales Branch Library – City of Albuquerque Public Library System." Its facade towered over the street, blonde brick and white concrete pediments, with deep-set metal-framed windows. With a different sign, it could have been a school. GMR admired school buildings. He heaved open one of the massive doors and ducked into the air conditioning. His eyes adjusted to the dimness of the library, and as he hesitated there, the librarian leaned over the counter to speak to him. "Hello, GMR. I thought you might come in today."

He stared up at her, her black hair drawn back with a clip, her eyes big behind the glasses. "Hi, Miss Parch."

"You left your card last time. I kept it for you." The boy mumbled something indistinct in reply and she talked on. "Let me see your hands." He held them out for inspection. "Pretty dirty. Why don't you head into the restroom and wash them before you touch the books."

"Okay." She reached over the counter, brushed his hair with her hand, first left then right, restored a part to his thatch. He flinched each time her hand swept across his scalp, but didn't move away. When she was done he headed back to the hall. The boy stopped at the water cooler, and drank deep. If he turned his head sideways he could barely see her: she watched him from across the room. Their eyes met – she jerked her attention back to the reading room. The boy shouldered his way into the men's room.

CHAPTER THREE

A TYPICAL FAT AMERICAN CAR of the working poor parked at the curb in front of an office building. Reverend Halvard's white knuckles clutched the steering wheel. Before he got out of the car and went in, Halvard wanted to remind himself of who he was. No one else could know, but he carried that sense of self all the time. It was only when he had to do something difficult, like standing up for himself that the Reverend needed reminding, a little bolstering. Now he had to beg the Convention for emergency funds for the leaking roof. Like a fool, he had already promised it to the church board.

He sat behind the wheel, behind the windscreen, behind his sunglasses, debating what was necessary and what was not. With a quiver, knowing it would feel good, he reached across and opened the glove compartment, dug under the paper that stuffed the glove box, under a small black bible with a red ribbon The gun in its carry holster, his trusted servant, appeared in his hand like a little sacrament. Drawing the shining engine of smoke and thunder, he cocked the nickel hammer and tossed the pistol from his right to his left hand and back. Dropping the hammer, he placed it back in the holster, and wedged it all in his waistband at his back, under the wrinkled seersucker jacket. Propped forward by the revolver's bite in his spine, the Reverend opened the door, ready.

———

AT FOUR FORTY-FIVE, REGINA STEPPED up with a little leap onto the platform behind the bar at Rip's. Tenn stripped off his apron and handed it to her. "I'll be back in a bit."

Her blue-black face split apart in a smile. "Sure thing, boss."

He slid out the back door into the alley and down to the street. He turned left and there to the side he caught a glimpse of movement in the lumberyard. He slowed. Peering into the darkness of one of the sheds, he thought he saw something, a big dog or a small person under the racks of lumber. "Hello, boy. Nice afternoon. Not too hot, not too cold." He heard no answer. Tenn shrugged and paced on.

Two blocks later Tenn marched up to the family bungalow. He turned in the gate and strode past the stucco wall down cracked concrete. The dirt of the yard trapped a reluctant yucca or two, but they had no lawn to maintain – only white dust and gravel. The second Tenn unlocked the front door, the smell of cornbread leaked out of the house onto the porch. It was a shotgun cottage: each room opened one after another onto that dark narrow hallway in a riffle of genteel poverty, washing up at the back door ahead. He could hear a pan lid clatter and a spoon strike metal on metal. "I'm home," he said, and shut the door.

Lavinia's neutral voice floated down the hall. "Go wash your hands."

Tenn did as he was bid. Then he turned into the kitchen, leaned against the door jamb. He studied his sister. A flowered dress with a white collar hung off her shoulders, a lime green apron edged in white ruffles wrapped about her. The style said large plump grand-mother, not this thin rawboned woman with wrinkled arms. The lid of the large soup pot came off, and he watched her elbow working as she stirred. Her back was as straight as a post.

The room was dense with bright rich smell – chicken, carrot, pepper, chili. He got down two glasses from the cupboard, broke ice cubes out of an aluminum tray. "Smells great, Lavinia. Sweetened tea?"

She turned from the stove to say, "Thank you, Tennyson. It's green chile stew tonight, with cornbread." She bent to draw the hot cornbread out of the oven.

"Sounds great, Lavinia. I'll fill bowls."

She glanced back at him, from the oven door and said, "That would be nice."

As he ladled out soup from the big pot, he said, "I saw Red Donnie today."

"Well …." His sister spoke towards the wall clock that hung in front of her as she flipped cornbread out onto a cooling rack. She might have said more, but it died in the moment.

He clacked the bowls onto the table and sat himself down. His mouth twitched to the side in a little frown. "He's a thoughtful man."

She turned to glance at him, enough that he caught sight of her pursed lips. "That man drinks a lot for a Christian."

"He can't drink much, Lavinia. He's either working or at home with his mother."

"He's changed his ways, Tennyson? He doesn't stop in two or three times a day?"

She slipped into her chair, hitching it forward. He cut the corn-bread on the cooling rack, placed a crumbling butter-yellow piece on each saucer on the table. Both of them sat erect in their seats and lifted the spoons all the way up to their lips without ducking their heads. They ate silently for awhile. Steam escaped from the bowls, carrying savory smell of vegetables and broth up into the room.

"I didn't bring him up so we could judge him."

She regarded her brother. "You're right, Tennyson. 'Judge not that ye be not judged.'"

He was quiet for a moment, relieved. "The stew is wonderful." He hadn't yet gotten to what he wanted to say. "Red Donnie is worried."

"About what?"

"About the boy." Lavinia raised a questioning eyebrow. "You know, the runaway that lives in the alley. GMR."

"People ought to have names, not initials."

"So, do you want to hear about it or not?"

"Sorry," she said. She reached over and patted his hand. "You go right ahead, and don't let your big sister bully you."

He took another bite, to space it out. He spoke, "Red Donnie thinks we should do something."

"Yes, we should." She cut more cornbread, nudged the tub of margarine across to him. "But why stop with this child? What about his brother and sisters?"

"I've thought some about the other children. Hopefully they'll be scooped up into Child Protective Services. The police will come out to the house one too many times, until it's too late to save the family. Then the kids will go into the system."

"Not everyone agrees with you that Child Services is a good thing. Maybe they have grandparents or relatives that can take them in. That would be best. Keep it in the family."

"Like the old days, Lavinia? At least this country has a safety net for children." He pointed with his spoon behind her on the wall. She had four framed pictures of children. A Latina girl stared out, big eyed and frizzy haired. A black boy stood at attention in front of a shack, appearing far too thin. An Asian girl crouched on the ground, wearing rags, a gap between her two teeth. A white child with a cloud of hair, hard to tell if boy or girl, gazed over its shoulder, with a hand in its mouth.

"You're talking about the children I sponsor? My babies have the Nuns. Your boy in the alley has no one."

"Maybe that's the point. This boy had the sense to get out. He's an independent little bugger."

"I wish you wouldn't use that word, Tennyson. At least not in this house."

"Sorry." The conversation lagged, strayed off to other things, then he circled back around. "The boy, he's already shown initiative. And that he's smarter than his parents. It would be a shame to force him back into that house, a house full of drunks.."

"Tennyson, you're as soft-hearted as an old woman."

"Not me. It's Red Donnie who has the soft spot."

She grinned a crooked little smile. "If you say so. How is work going today?"

"So far so good. Nice steady flow of customers all afternoon. I think sometimes I see the whole village at least once a week, including the churches. Well, not the ministers, but surely the deacons."

"Rip's, the village center." She had a dryness in her tone.

He agreed with her words, if not the sentiment, "At least Tuesdays through Saturdays. Roger Kyber came in. His mom is still doing poorly. He hasn't opened his repair place for maybe three weeks. He pretty much stays at home with her, or is busy driving her up to the hospital."

"I'm glad you got a chance to see him. I never thought much of Roger, but he has certainly done proud taking care of his mother."

"Yes. It used to be the other way around. She minded after all of us, both in Texas and here after the farms failed. Now he's the one who has to—"

"She was stricter than Mother, harder on you than her own son, I thought."

He snorted. "Guess I deserved it. We should go over and see Mrs. Kyber, maybe Monday when I'm closed. Roger didn't think it would be very long before the hospice people come in. It doesn't look good. Are you done with those, Big Sister?" He dipped his head towards her bowl and spoon.

She wiped her mouth with a napkin. "Yes, yes I am."

He got up and stacked the dishes, carried them over to the sink. "Well, I better get back to work. Thanks for supper."

"You're welcome, Tennyson."

"You coming down later?"

"To the Den of Iniquity, your Sea of Sin?"

"No, just to Rip's"

"Maybe. I'll decide after Father Tom's show."

He nodded, and trudged down the hall. On the porch, he got a key ring off his belt, and threw the deadbolt on the front door. The neighborhood was changing.

BACK AT RIP'S, TENN HOPPED up onto his riser behind the counter. Regina cocked her eye at him and said, "I packed the place for you, Tenn. Now it's your job to not drive them away."

He gazed out over Rip's. The bar stools were filled, all but one, by men who hunched forward on their elbows over their drinks. The last barstool held a tiny Hispaño woman opposite Regina, with a tall red drink parked on a mat in front of her. A couple at a table at the front under the ribbon window held hands, gazed at each other. "Yes. Thanks, Regina. You've filled the place up." He went to the register and got out a twenty and a ten. "Here you go, another hour off the books."

Regina handed him the apron, caught the folded money like a butterfly and made it disappear. She said, "See you tomorrow night, then." She waved goodbye to her friend and then added, "Our adulterers need a refill, poor things." She tipped her head at the couple in front, and rolled out, her thin legs swaying the upturned derrière in goodbye.

He cast his professional gaze about Rip's. Three of the men on their stools worked on a lackadaisical argument as they stared into the mirror of the bar at each other. Striding past them, clacking a bowl of bar nuts down in front of them, he heard, "Now, baseball, that's a real American sport."

"Naah, baseball is as dumb as dirt and more boring. Basketball, that's your true American sport."

"What do you know about it. You're white."

"I ain't as white as you are."

He inspected the other four men more closely – they had the pale, sagging faces of dedicated serial drinkers. He knew three of them well and they knew him. Their car keys rested in front of them: he scooped them up, dropped them in a mug by the cash register, and poured again for them.

Unbidden he made up another Crown and Coke and a white Zin, popped them on a tray, and whisked them over to the couple in the window. He hovered. The couple jerked their hands back with a start, stared up at him.

"Rhonda, Julio. Nice night out, isn't it?" He distributed new napkins, placed the drinks down, and picked up the empties. He glanced at her and sized up a small person: she was died blonde and worn down at the edges.

Rhonda laughed, a sweet sound. "We're not sitting on the patio at Anton's. We won't know if it's pleasant out until we leave."

"Well, it's a nice night because you're here, Rhonda."

Julio spoke, "Always a zalamero, Tenn. It's okay, man, we love coming here. Where else could we sit in the quiet and talk to each other." Julio jittered in his chair, a bone-thin squinty-eyed Hispaño, intense, as if animated by electricity.

"You mean ....?"

"What happens at Rip's stays at Rip's."

"Well, it's good to have you come in under any terms."

CHAPTER FOUR

R IGHT AT DAWN, GMR TIPTOED onto the back porch, crouching a bit as he did so. He raised his head enough to peer in the back door, through the fly-spattered glass. His gaze made out a woman in a chair, her back to him and her head down on the table. With his mother Intienda asleep in the kitchen, he couldn't go in through the back. The boy tried the front door next. He retrieved a key from under a rock, then noticed the door yawned open. He tipped his head, inched it between the frame and the scratched, chipped door, and peered into the living room. A man curled up on the couch snorted on the inhale and whistled on the exhale. It wasn't GMR's father.

Someone had left a dusty lawnmower at the corner of the house. He wheeled it around the side and over to a window, scraping the house a bit, pausing to see if anyone heard. When no face appeared at the window, he crawled up on the mower and carefully forced up the sash. With a lunge he got his chest up on the sill and slithered headfirst into the room. The room held four beds: he landed on the floor between two of them.

Amy, little sister, lay in the bed to the right. He peered at her asleep there, and decided she didn't look any thinner than the last time he had seen her. Her stuffed bear was on the floor – he grabbed it by the arm and nestled it on the bed by her hand. In the bed to his left sprawled his older sister, Juanita. She had gone to sleep in her makeup, and had smeared tracks across the pillow. The smudges on her face and the open mouth made her appear younger than Amy.

Bud lay in a third bed. GMR stayed as far as he could from the fifteen-year-old – he shied away, not turning his back on Bud.

The fourth bed had been his – all the stuff piled on it proved his brother and sisters knew he was gone. He crept through the room, spotted the crumpled beer can that lay by Bud's bed, eased the bedroom door open and snuck down the hall, past the open door of his parents' bedroom. When the boy slipped into the utility room, he swung the door shut, careful to tug up on the knob to avoid that horrible creak.

Here the family had an extra refrigerator, a washer and a dryer, and three hampers. The boy first searched the fridge to see if it held anything he wanted. The only contents were beer and three bottles – vodka, margarita mix, an Irish Cream that wasn't cream at all. He dug around in a hamper until he found some of his clothes, laundered but left in a tangle with those of all the others. He kicked off his shoes, stripped off what he wore, and tugged on the new, wrinkled clothes, burying the dirty ones in a pile heaped on the floor.

He paused in the door of the kitchen to spy on his mother Intienda. On this morning she was fully dressed, except for one shoe. Her face lay partially on a bag of chips, partially on a lid of a bean dip can: she snored softly, breathing easy. The bottle stood empty by her hand: her zippered case hid in her lap. No chance to check the pantry and the refrigerator.

His father was in no better shape than his mother. He sprawled across his bed in his jeans and T-shirt, boots still on. GMR's nose wrinkled – the sour smell of vomit permeated the still air, but he couldn't see the puddle.

The boy decided he could escape out the front door rather than the window, so he slipped into the living room. The coffee table supported a mountain range of bottles and cans, but he guessed they didn't come from a single night. The table also held an open cereal box, and the boy scooped that up, holding it against his chest. On the couch, the stranger spotted earlier continued to snore. A second man lay in the stuffed chair by the front door, close to the getaway path. GMR stared at this man, intent on easing past him. He slipped around the half-open door. That's when his foot struck the beer can. It leapt forward and caromed off the wall, a table leg. The boy snatched the door shut behind him and sprinted down the front walk. He heard a shout behind him, "Hey kid!"

CHAPTER FIVE

At four thirty in the afternoon, an old fashioned alarm clock with a hammer and two bells clanged on a glass countertop, juddering around under its own impetus. Richard Martin jerked awake. Angry, he struck at the clock with a large soft hand. Muttering, "Son of a bitch!" he gazed about the store and shook himself, like an elephant flapping its ears and getting up out of the muddy river.

Ponderous, stretching, scratching, he rose from the stool, breathing a heavy sigh as he brushed away some dandruff and a couple of gray hairs from the counter. Groaning, he bent to pick up the book that had fallen to the floor. "Whitman. I should make an alarm from you, my friend.

Awake, awake

For I am all men!"

He moved out from behind his glass cases into the room and to the door. His feet were shod in slippers: his heels had broken them down in back. Surrounded by the dust and the clutter of his pawnshop he locked up and turned off the "Open" sign. The dust had its own faint smell – an odor of stale bread with a whiff of ozone. With indifference he appraised the treasure trove – a complete banquet set from a failing restaurant, a pristine MOPAR four-barrel carburetor, a brass chandelier, guitars, stereos, and other regrets of his neighbors' financial decisions. "King of all I see," he intoned. "Prince of the Abandoned."

Back behind the counter, the Prince reached down and extracted a paper bag with a bottle in it, and poured from the bottle into a wine glass with a chipped base, setting it on his open ledger. His stubby finger opened the cash register. Counting out the bills and change, he made a notation in the ledger, and then hauled out his book of yellow and white slips to total the tickets for the day. In the margin of a newspaper he added and subtracted with a pencil. "Two hundred dollars of new stock. One fourteen and seventy-six cents left in the till. Eighty-six dollars behind. That figures." He gulped down a substantial slurp from the glass, shuddered, and waited for the acrid fumes to race up into his sinuses.

His fingers fumbled through tags hanging from the rifles behind their lock bars. "July, July, August ... July, September. Here's one – June 5th." He did the same for a display of handguns below glass, then locked the display down under a metal cover. He went to the phone and called across town.

"Herman, this is Richard – Good, good, how are you? – I got two more nines and a thirty aught six you can have. – I don't know. I paid out what the book said, minus the margin. – You take a look at them and tell me what you'll give me for them – Naah, I hate the damn things. – I pawn 'em, I redeem 'em, and I sell 'em on as soon as possible." He listened without much interest – his mouth hung slack and his breath soughed stertorously. "Tomorrow, sure. We'll have a drink, okay?" Richard had a drink right then, tossed off the last of the liquid ether in the wine glass. He turned off the lights, shuffled through the dark and cluttered back room, and armed the alarm.

Rip's screen door waited only two doors down the alley from the pawnshop. Richard lumbered through the back checking neither left nor right. As he passed through the package liquor section he stooped down with a long sigh, and picked up a bottle of vodka off the bottom row, the cheap row. He grunted as he straightened, and with deep unsteady breaths, shuffled into the bar area and sagged onto a stool at the counter, placing the bottle he'd chosen on the bar top.

Tenn leaned on one elbow and polished a glass. With a flourish of the towel, he racked it above his head, and shot a glance at his friend, "You're looking good, Richard."

"Well, I'm not deceased yet. You appear in the pink yourself, Tennyson."

Tenn inclined his head in acknowledgement and asked, "Need an eye opener?"

"My thirst is the thirst of the desert, of the lizard and the snake, of the empty wash awaiting early spring rain."

Tenn picked up Richard's bottle of vodka and wiggled it into a paper bag. "As you know, we don't control the rain, but the alcohol deliveries are regular. The usual?"

"With my undying gratitude."

"I'll add it to the tab." Tenn dumped ice, milk, vodka, and Kahlua into a shaker, made a clattering sound, and poured it into a squat glass.

Richard coughed into his large hand. "And whom do we expect in tonight, and what salacious gossip about them do we know?"

"What was your question again?" asked Tenn.

"Who can we gossip about and stare at?"

"Well, Rhonda and Julio are going through a bad patch, and they sneak in most evenings early. You can gossip about them."

"A bad patch? They have each other."

"Not really. Julio is bound to a bitch of a wife, and his Catholicism won't let him do anything about it. Rhonda won't break up her marriage because of the kids."

Richard held up two fingers, made the sign of the cross. "We bless the American nuclear family. Glow-in-the-dark toxic."

"It's just the way it is, Richard. Parents wear out. Teenagers go all independent, especially if they have a car."

"You ever have a car when you were a kid?"

"Of course not. If I remember the story right, you had too many cars, and the police caught you in one of them."

"Ahh, the folly of my youth. Misspent childhood. Juvy Hall, residence extraordinaire. Service to the community—"

Tenn held up his hand. "Stop. If you keep it up, I'll have to go talk to another customer."

"But I am more than a customer. I am an investor. I deposit my time, my talent, my money into this small establishment, and what do I get?"

"You get a bar tab and White Russians, and no other bar down in the Bosque would give you a drink like that." Tenn tapped the side of Richard's drink, made the ice chink.

"Alas, that is true. We've sunk to the level of American beers, all of which claim to be 'Light.'"

Tenn said, "Be right back," and strode down the bar to refill a glass of light beer. He polished the counter in front of the customer and exchanged some words. By the time he reached his post in front of his friend, Richard's glass stood empty, accusing, shoved back to Tenn's side.

"Another?"

"God, yes. But tell everyone you forced it on me."

31

By nine, Rip's had filled up. Tenn had four tables in use, where people drank tequila or bourbon and coke for the most part, and a lined-up bar where the clients nursed beer or vodka. The locals knew enough to come up to the counter for refills, but he did have a table of newcomers that reclined in their chairs and waited for him to come serve them. Tenn saw the rest of his customers casting disapproval their way.

The rule-breakers numbered five, three men and two women. They dressed in that monied office-casual seen all over the West – khaki instead of worsted wool, starched polos rather than white button-downs, and loafers rather than dress shoes.

Harry Weissman said to Richard, "An even bet they drove up in three cars minimum, and that at least two of the cars are German."

Richard replied, "I am betting on sniffy little hybrids. Observe, they have chosen wine, both red and white. Tennyson's finest, not the cheap stuff – real corks."

Harry rubbed his bald head. "Why does Tenn let these types of folks in?"

"I assume there is a profit motive, my cheap beer-drinking crony. He would delight in Rip's transformation into a professionals' watering hole."

"Quiet, Tenn's headed our way."

"And that should concern me?"

Tenn clomped down his riser behind the bar, checked out the drinks and talk. The people on barstools concentrated on sports and weather. Tenn dipped and sampled the dialogue like a dragonfly touching water.

The most charged conversation revolved on politics – two women were running for Governor in New Mexico. Richard held forth, waved his glass in the air, spaced his words with importance and weight. "Consider the last famous woman who was a Governor in our fair nation. She couldn't hack it, so she resigned. Said it was the press's fault, but you know she had bollixed it up and was getting out before a God-awful moment of public discovery."

Harry Weissman replied, "Richard, you are so full of it. I can't figure out if you're against that particular woman because you're a liberal, or if you're a right-wing woman-hater."

"The term, little man, is misogynist."

"For which, liberal or woman-hater?"

"Gender, of course, my illiterate friend. As for politics, I am a Libertarian, which means 'Leave Me Alone.'"

Harry shot a heads-up look at the others to announce his up-coming triumph. "I notice most people want to leave you alone." His audience gave out hoots and applause, and Tenn caught a sharp stare from Richard as he himself grinned. Deferring any rebuke from Richard, Tenn conveyed glasses of water and a bowl of bar nuts out to his newcomers. As he hopped down to the floor, he heard a customer ask, "Has anyone seen GMR today?" Harry answered, "In a dumpster behind Julio's. He's moving around fine, looked okay."

When Tenn returned to his post, Harry leaned across the dark shiny top and asked him, "So, how can you tell when Richard is drunk?" Harry glanced at the behemoth on the stool beside him.

Tenn rubbed the side of his nose with his forefinger. "Is this a riddle, like 'Why does the chicken cross the road?'"

"No, I was serious. I don't know that I've ever seen Richard drunk."

Richard prodded Harry's elbow with a fat finger. "You misapprehend the situation, Harold. You have seldom seen me sober. I determined some time ago – I think it was during the sixth foster home – that intoxication is the natural state of a philosophical man. Since then, I have found that alcohol is the proper stimulant and have adopted it – much as the Welsh bard did – forsaking all others."

Tenn nodded in agreement. "He's right Harry. What's the use of getting sober, when you gotta do it all over again?"

Harry asked, "That's a song lyric isn't it?"

Tenn smiled to himself.

Harry wasn't done with Richard yet. "What about Sunday?"

Richard said, "But you're Jewish, Harry. It's Shabbat for you, not our Sunday, right?"

"No, I don't have anything against drinking on Saturday. It was my thought that *you'd* be in trouble on Sundays because the bars are closed until noon."

"True, but precautions can be taken." Richard decided to leave it at that. Jerking his head backwards, he asked Tenn, "What's the story about them?"

"You mean the five at the flat-top?"

"Yeees."

Tenn polished the chipped dark enamel that covered the bar top. His silver hair had a blue and red halo from the neon behind him. "I think they're soaking up a little bit of local color. I would prefer you two avoid giving them your version of color."

"We get it," said Harry. "You'd really and truly like to see them back in here again."

Richard spoke, "Yes, the gentrification of Rip's. Hangout of the rich and famous."

"Yeah, what he said." Harry frowned at the yuppie table. "They're way too good-looking for Rip's. Rip himself wouldn't like it."

Tenn diverted the discussion. "There is no Rip. There never has been a Rip. It's unlikely there ever will be a Rip."

CHAPTER SIX

A SHED SQUATTED DEEP IN a backyard, heating up from the midmorning sun. Some factory had made it out of cheap metal that had once been painted green and sold it through a big-box store; now it had gone gray, rust streaked and dented here and there. The door had a ramp down into the ragged grass, and a padlock. The shed had an open window on the backside, a foot from the cinderblock wall that ran around the yard. GMR could wiggle through, if he sat on the wall and dangled his feet inside. The next step was perilous: he could scoot down onto the sill, bend backwards, and slip in. The metal windowsill would rake his back.

The interior held a jumble of tools heaped on the stained concrete floor, and the air smelled of gasoline. A lawnmower filled up the space in front of the door. The little room baked. In the corner someone had thrown down a canvas tarp. GMR lay on top of most of it, with a flap drawn over his body.

In repose, he appeared broken. One leg hung out from under the tarp, thin and dirty. Dark hair stuck up in various directions from his head, and his face had a dusky, gray tan. The boy's mouth hung open and saliva dampened the tarp under his face. A fly, tranquility itself, droned overhead, bumping the window glass soft, easy.

Outside, down the alley, Helen Parch's car waited idling, the morning delayed, the fantasy lingering. Behind darkened glass, blown on by the AC, her pudgy white soft hand stroked her bare thigh. A number of stories could play out ahead. The boy could have gone somewhere else last night. The boy could have already left the shed. The boy could soon get in the car.

CHAPTER SEVEN

ILENE MCKENNET DROPPED INTO HER recliner and heard it complain under her weight. She waited for a stillness to return to the room, to the chair, to her hams. Time didn't count in that living room; the air was thick and somnolent. The room was hot, just the way she liked it, hot enough that she sweated in penance. In the kitchen the preacher echoed forth from the radio, his phrasing taut, compelling, and as rhythmic as a hymn. He preached on King Ahab and Ahab's chariot of redemption. Here in the front room though, on a doily-strewn couch, the Devil reclined, wizened and smelling like pine tar. "I knew Ahab. Good man overall, damn him!" the Devil said. "But I really knew Jezebel, his wife."

"I bet you knew her," she said.

"Jezzie gave in to me, as easy as kiss my hand. Woman loved luxury, she did."

"We don't all give in."

"You will." The Devil laughed, and his breath had that smell of sap backed up by a dark smoky taint. "You'll give in, because you want it too much, don't you?"

"Wanting is the thing, isn't it? If you can get me to need something, soon I need everything."

"And what do you lust after, my dearest? Is it the food? Pie? Butter dripping off a fresh baked biscuit? Tender, juicy pig perched on your fork, kissing your lips with tiny squeals?"

Her mouth made the tiniest smack. She swallowed. "No thanks. Food is but a fuel that fires God's engines."

"Yeah, there's some truth in that, at least for you. You *want* food, but you *need* something more. That chocolate cake is a layer of dream on top of real desire, a consolation for a truer loss. Hmm, what is it you need? You want – want the man, don't you? Ah, the other, the beloved, the two-backed beast. That intimacy, that oneness with another being, that entanglement of spirit and flesh."

"You're a dirty, dirty thing, aren't you? Disgusting."

"You made me, Ilene. I am but your creation."

"God made you. And threw you into the pit."

"True enough, as far as it goes. But enough about me. I can give you what you need, you know. All hundred-and-twenty pounds of him, all those wrinkles and sagging skin, all that black Magyar hair. All of Cheezsy Milosovich Brezinski. And then!" He folded his hands and crossed his hooves.

"Then what?"

"You become of this world, my world."

"I shall surrender up this corporeal world unto the demands of my Savior Jesus Christ."

"Those words are so preacher-like! That's how I know you'll give in, because they're just something you parrot." He laughed with a sawing sound, "Heh, heh, heh."

She shook her head, "No." He would not have her, at least not today. She sighed and reached up to touch the ring of sweat beneath her arm. Even facing the Devil, she still had to take care of ordinary life. Time to get to work at the Key to the Kingdom. She shifted, about to stand, and a fart escaped.

The Devil cackled, "There's your corporeal world, all right."

AT THE END OF A long day, Red Donnie trudged down the sidewalk in front of the strip. His big feet shuffled down past Cut 'n Curl, Julio's and Rip's to his own store, Key to the Kingdom. He reached up for the door handle, dropped his hand, reached again.

Inside, he said, "Hi, Mom, it's me. I'm back. I brought Slushies." He could smell the oil from his keys, and that burnt-sparks smell of the grinder. He opened up the paper bag.

Ilene and Red Donnie had arranged the front of the store into three aisles, lined with supermarket shelves they bought from a failed convenience store. A sparse number of books, maybe two hundred selections in all, spread through the space, arranged with corners trued up just so. Ilene dedicated one aisle to paper fold-out dioramas of key biblical scenes. Along the back wall, Red Donnie kept all the mechanical bits and pieces of the key business, on shelves, in drawers, in trays, and loose on the countertop.

She perched on the barstool behind the glass counter, a cash register to her left and a little TV to the right, coax for the cable hanging limply off the back. She broke her gaze away from the TV – the Christian Network, as usual. Smiling, she said, "I thought you'd never get here."

"Sorry. A guy locked his keys in his car this morning, and didn't call till he got off work, right in the middle of the afternoon rush! I got into his vehicle easy, but the drive back and forth this time of day...."

"That's okay." He set the Slushy on the counter. "Thanks, Don."

She ducked her head, seized the straw in her lips and slurped for a long three-count. "It's a show about Galilee."

He asked, "Haven't we seen that one?" He shambled around the glass counter to park on his locksmith's stool, at an angle to her TV.

She waved a hand in dismissal; the flesh under her upper arm jiggled. "Probably. You can tell me about your day and we'll let it run in background." She turned the sound down, some.

"Well, before you got here, I cut some keys. The usual thing: renters with new roommates the landlord doesn't know about. And I bumped into Tenn. He sends his regards."

She sucked on the straw. "That man does the Devil's work and you know it."

"Oh, Tenn is okay. He's knocked around the world a bit and ended up tending bar. He takes a personal interest in his customers, and somebody else would manage the bar if it wasn't him."

"Knocked around." She turned the sound back up. He winced. "You can't make excuses for what a man does. He either walks righteous, or he walks the other path."

On the set, images of desert and date orchards rolled on, carried by portentous narration. The small screen showed a crypt – the camera dived inside into the dark – wobbly, green tinged. She raised a white hand towards the burial site and turned the volume down. "I saw the Devil again today."

"Jeez, Mom, I wish you wouldn't say things like that. Not even to be funny."

"It wasn't funny. Or not funny hah-hah."

"So what did the Devil want?" He shot her a glance, then scrutinized the tile on the floor between them.

"Same as always. My soul. Satan is a persistent force, a compulsion of evil to destroy."

"And a sharp dresser."

She heard a snicker from the stockroom, the scrape of a chair. She thought she could smell creosote. "Don't belittle Him. Otherwise He will visit you." The Devil was here, and Don didn't even notice. She wagged a finger at Donnie. "Don't tempt Him."

He picked up his Slushy, turned it in his hand, considered it. "So, Ma, why should he be after you more than anyone else?"

"It's hard to stay righteous. He knows that." Now the Devil flat-out laughed, and an echo followed the hoot out of the store-room. Maybe she could test it, test what her son could see. "Did you hear that? Something in the stockroom? Could you check for me, dear?"

He sloped off to the door, stuck his head around the corner, scanned the small space. "Nothing here but our junk. Hot in here, and stinks. I can smell the tar from the roof."

Hopeless. No one would ever believe her. "Anything else today at the shop?" She turned the volume back up.

"Brother Jones from the church came in. He'd put off picking up those hymnbooks forever, but he finally showed up. Now we can bill for them."

Over the sound of a TV choir raising its voice in song, she said, "Is that all? We can't make a living off one customer a day."

"Oh, the emergency calls are where we make the money." He gargled in the bottom of his Slushy, tried to get more ice up the straw. "Remember the runaway I was telling you about?"

She raised her voice over the TV, "The boy behind the store?"

"Yeah, well, around."

"Don't mumble, dear."

He pitched his voice up, "People in the neighborhood are taking an interest in him."

"Call the police, or Child Welfare. That's what you should do."

"But what happens then, Mom? They'll probably take him back home and turn him over to his parents."

"And that's a bad thing?"

"I don't think they're very good parents, Mom."

"They can't do their duty if he's not in the home."

He let that one alone. As he poked at the ice in his cup with the straw, he said, "I met the boy's parents once." They watched through the segment on the Dome of the Rock. From his stool, he saw the TV as a dusty, battered cube, and the Dome could just as well have been St. Peters.

An ad for Crystal Cathedral Ministries spun out its come-hither. "Are you going to tell me about them?"

"Oh, nice enough, I guess. They weren't getting along very well, and they sure looked like they lead a hard life."

"There's nothing wrong with hard work."

"No, Mom, I mean I think they drink a lot."

"The Church would help with that. Perhaps our Mission people could go talk to them."

"What would you think about – well, what if the boy lived with us for awhile, till we got the situation sorted out?"

A long silence, and he turned his eyes up to meet his mother's stare. He ducked his head back down to his Slushy.

With a laborious shake of her head, her mouth turned down in an oxbow, his mother said, "This isn't California, and this isn't the Summer of Love."

"I don't think I follow."

"You want to help this child? Don't start a commune here. Call the authorities, or take him down to the Shelter. Do it the upright way. I've been through your friends moving in before."

"That was way back in 1969. And this is one person, an eight-year-old boy."

"No, I can't get comfortable with that, Don. You'd have a marijuana smoker under our roof next, or a junkie off the corner. God Himself Knows."

He muttered, "It's *my* apartment."

"Don't mumble dear."

—⁓—

ALL OF SUMMER'S CHARACTER MANIFESTED as a hot June day, a Tuesday. Regina always parked at the end of the block and entered Rip's from the back.

Today, though, she ended up a block away – the curbs were littered with old clunkers. Her ancient Impala eased up to park. She rolled the windows down a crack and unfolded a reflector on top of the dash, up under the windshield. She switched off the air conditioning and the car.

Swinging her legs out from under the wheel, she viewed her thighs, shining in hose. Too big, especially with those pipestem shins below. The wheel and the seat-back got her up onto perilous heels, and she leaned back in to get her takeout. Her legs scissored her down the alley through the dust. She heard a scuffle sound to the left. She stared under a loading dock. Back where the deck grating cast down a grid of black and white, she saw a mane of black hair, and a face with two large eyes. "If I can see you, you can see me. Come on out and talk."

The boy crawled out on his hands and knees, and stood up. He flicked his eyes from right to left. Would he run? After a small hesitation, he thrust his hands into his pockets and hunched his shoulders.

"We've met before. I'm Regina Talmadge."

"'Lo."

Where was the long introduction that Tenn talked about? "I work in the bar. You know, over there. Not as far down as where your house is."

"You leave food out. On the step."

"No, that's the Manager who leaves you food. Are you hungry now?" The boy's head moved up and down – a bobble-head. "I'll get you something if you want." They trod up the alley together, with a safe gap between them. She didn't say anything until they reached Rip's back door. "Is a cheese sandwich okay?"

"Yes."

She kept the door from banging to avoid any startling noise. She got Tenn's paper bag from beneath the counter, fished a bottle of water out from the cooler and scooted back. GMR waited in the sun in the center of the alley. Regina thumped down on the stoop, placed the bag and the bottle on the concrete at arm's length. The boy sidled over, picked them up, and plunked down – four feet away, out of reach. Not too close, not too far.

He opened the bag, fished out the sandwich in a ziplock, and dug it out. His jaws worked for a while. Chewing away he opened the bottle of water – twisted at the cap in an awkward manner. He drank deep, and in his haste, water dripped off his chin.

"So, when you don't eat here, where do you eat?"

"The Mexican restaurant. Mr. Julio sometimes gives me something."

"But you don't always eat there."

"No."

"Are you getting food out of the dumpsters?"

He cast her a glance, focused on the dirt at her feet. "Uh huh." The boy turned back to his sandwich. "Don't tell anyone."

She made no promise. "Must not be all that nice."

"It's okay. Kind of smelly."

She wrinkled her nose. Rip's dumpster near them breathed out its own tangled, beery aroma. "Do you eat smelly food?"

"Sure. You can't tell if it's the food that smells, or – you know...."

"Yeah. Could be a problem."

The boy gazed straight at her. "I don't eat it if it's got bugs. That's the rule."

They sat still. The distant sibilance of traffic lulled the air, the town, lulled them. The boy dug out another sandwich. As he stuffed the last bite into his mouth, Regina made her offer. "Maybe you ought to eat here more often. What type of food do you like?"

"I like burgers."

"I do too." Liked them too much – she had to vomit them up, after she enjoyed the grease, the mustard, the onion. Get it out, keep it off.

Regina set the hook. "Come here tomorrow, and knock on the back door. I'll have a burger for you, and we'll warm it up in the microwave. I'll also have a bag of chips."

He popped up like a jack-in-the-box. "Okay." He took a step, wavered, half turned.

She asked, "So what do we say when someone gives us something?"

"Thank you."

"You're welcome. See you tomorrow." She rose and dusted off the back of her dress, turned to go in.

"See you." The boy sloped off, away from his house.

———

REGINA SAUNTERED SLOW THROUGH THE package liquor section, a frown on her face, and plunked down on a barstool. She hooked her heels up on the scarred wooden rung that held the stool together. Tenn stood back behind the bar, at parade-rest, pointed at her lunch on the counter in its takeout bag, and raised an eyebrow.

She said, "We're sharing lunch today. Do you want soup or salad?"

Tipping his head, he glanced under the bar. "Huh. No brown paper bag."

She handed him both his paper sack with the empty baggies and an empty plastic bottle. "GMR ate your sandwiches."

"Anything else here you want to give away? Drinks? The furniture?"

"Oh, shut up and pick. Soup or salad?"

Tenn dropped ice in a tall tumbler, mostly filled it with Coke, and added two shots of rum and a swizzle stick. "I'll take soup, unless it's cauliflower. You know, you feed a stray, pretty soon you got a pet."

"This pet needs a bath. He smells pretty ripe. That sweat smell kids get in their hair."

CHAPTER EIGHT

INTIENDA WHITTINGTON STOOD AT THE stove, a pan of sizzling Spam before her. Singed pork smell rose up around her, meaty with a vague chemical vapor. Tight capris made her ass look big, but the stretch shirt showed off a thin waist and compelling large breasts with all their cleavage. Glistening dark hair hung down around her cheap dime-store reading glasses and outlined her sour mouth.

Three children ringed the table behind her, slumped down, certain not to talk to each other. She reached up in the cupboard and got out a bag of chips and a squeeze bottle of mustard, and dumped all on the table between them. The breadbox provided a loaf of white bread. "Juanita," she said. Juanita hunched over texting on a pink phone, her black hair falling over the screen. "Juanita, pay attention. Get the pickle relish from the refrigerator. Get out three glasses and the milk."

Juanita shoved the phone in her back pocket and moped over to the refrigerator. Her jeans fit her low and tight, showed the shape of the phone on the bottom curve of her small butt. Returning, she clattered three plastic cups down on the table and filled them with milk. Bud, without comment, snatched his and continued to flip through the car magazine in his lap. A do-rag covered his head, and his spindly shanks sprouted out of his black baggy shorts, ending in huge white trainers emblazoned with the Swoosh. His pale forehead was wrinkled up in greed for a car, his eyebrows severe.

Amy grasped her cup with both hands and drank, dribbling some milk down her chin. Intienda said to Juanita, "Look, now. Look what she did. You should be helping her." Intienda grabbed a paper towel and hovered over Amy, mopping up the milk.

Juanita replied to the criticism, "Gee, and isn't she seven after all?" The crescent downturn of her mouth rolled out her lip.

"That's enough, Juanita. She needs our help. Our little pobrecita." The laundry room rasped out an alarm as Intienda finished frying the Spam. She poured the contents of the pan onto a paper plate and set it on the table. "Juanita, the laundry is ready. Move it to the drier, por favor." Intienda built a sandwich for Amy as Juanita wandered into the next room.

Bud still stared at the magazine, waiting for his sister to trudge back in. They squabbled over the mustard, but they slammed the sandwiches together and distributed the chips quick enough.

In three minutes, they all had finished their lunch, while Intienda watched. "Juanita, make us floats." Juanita set out four more cups – she threw a wild glance at Bud when he voluntarily went to the fridge and got out ice cream and root beer.

He said, "It's okay. It's not like I'll make it a habit. Move over."

Juanita flashed him a quick smile, one so brief it might not have happened. She scooped ice cream into the glasses; Bud opened three cans of root beer one after the other as he filled the cups. For Intienda's, he strode over to the cupboard by the stove, got down the Kahlua and added an inch of coffee liqueur. Without comment he handed it to his mother.

Intienda flopped into the chair beside her youngest, Amy. She ran her hand over the girl's hair as she held a large spoon out to the child. "Here go, baby," she said, and gave the girl a slurp of ice cream. Gathering her sleeve over her palm, Intienda wiped the crusts of dried tears from the small folds of the child's eyes and the line of snot from under her short nose.

Bud lolled in his chair, sullen and discontented. For no real reason he said to his sister, "Juanita, you're getting fat. You should give me your float, or what's left of it."

"You just shut up." Juanita hunched her shoulders over the float, and licked the spoon in a provocative way. She tilted her head back, simpered past the spoon.

"Mucho chanchita." Bud made snuffling noises, and held the end of his nose up with his middle finger.

"Mom!" said Juanita, without turning away from her brother.

Intienda shut off the baiting. "William Alexander, you hush now, and leave your sister alone. You're making tu madre's head hurt."

"Gotta go," Bud said. He got up and made off for the back door. His shoelaces trailed behind him like long blue worms. As he opened the screen, he said, "Later."

"Where you going, muchacho?"

"Out." The screen banged shut behind him.

"Juanita, take your sister into the front room; see if she wants to color in her coloring books."

The girl stood up, held out her hand, "C'mon Amy. Lets go play." They shuffled into the hallway, the teenager and the little round-headed girl.

Intienda wearily rose from the table. She poured more Kahlua into her cup and eased back down into her chair. She brought her elbows up onto the table to light a cigarette. First she teased it up out of the pack, caressed it with her hand, then placed it in her mouth, like placing the wafer on the tongue. She rolled the wheel on the lighter and stared into the flame. Finally she inhaled while the flame sucked into the white tube, held it, let it out with a long sigh. The husband at work. Her first born out on the street with los ladrónes. Juanita turning into a slut, and poor Amy. Better her other son stay away – she didn't have time for him. Bratty little mierda.

She gazed past the table-top clutter out into the back yard. She couldn't really drink until Whit came home. And couldn't do the other. It didn't hurt yet.

CHAPTER NINE

THE ONE THING THE ROOM had going for it was a king-size bed. Richard lay on his back in the center of it, on top of a field of rumpled sheets. Inert and insensible, draped in boxers and a sleeveless T-shirt, humanity run-down and given-up. The alarm jangled and he grunted. In five minutes, it clamored again. His body heaved up and swung its feet and legs over the side of the bed. Into the silence of the room he spoke, "If life is worth living, then it's also worth sleeping through." He got up, left the sheets, several small books, and a bottle behind in a cotton maelstrom.

Shaved and showered, he fished a heavy glass tumbler out from the kitchen cupboard, poured an inch of vodka into it from the bottle on the counter, and drank it off. A shudder wracked his shoulders, forcing out a little quiver of a noise, a vodka vocalization. He eased the glass down, and waited for the warming in his chest. "Eh! That is the sweet milk of mother's love, the happy accident of the distiller's art, the morning's redemption – all wrapped up into one." Holding up two fingers in benediction, he said, "Alexander Pope knew it all. Blessed is he who can unconcernedly find hours, days, and years, slide soft away in health of body, peace of mind, and the quiet by day."

Tugging on a sweater with unraveling cuffs, he proceeded to the door. "Well, then, I'm bound to work, to sell off life's small pleasures." He swayed out of his apartment, forgetting to lock the door behind him. On the stairs, he said, "I've got to stop talking to myself. The trouble is, I'm the most interesting person I know."

———

SOULFUL THOUGHT HE WAS PRETTY interesting: in fact, Harry knew Soulful to talk about himself a lot. Harry opened the door to AAA Slammer Relief, and entered what he called "The House of Linoleum." Soulful had linoleum on the floor. Linoleum covered the desktops. Linoleum crept halfway up the wall, and a paint that mimicked linoleum climbed on up to the top cornice. Linoleum in mass quantities has its own smell, even after years of use. Harry had grown tired of it, and of Soulful's monologues. Still, Harry couldn't beat the deal.

On the phone, feet on the desk, Soulful waved at Harry. Even in the chair he resembled a tall muscled Thor, blond, sharp dressed, perfect hair. Harry scurried past the big Swede. His relief was soon sent packing; Soulful slammed the phone down and swiveled his chair around to Harry. "Weissman! Good to see you. Your phone has been ringing off the hook."

"Well, either business is good or the creditors are angry."

"Yeah, I know about *creditors*. But that reminds me of the time I was chasing a skipper across town, and found him hiding at his brother-in-law's."

"So?" Here we go again. Harry turned half away.

"So his brother-in-law ran a savings and loan that was trying to repossess my car. Pretty funny huh? The skipper had my money, as it were, and I was in a car paid for by his family."

"I didn't think you chased your own runners."

"Sometimes, when money is tight. Nowadays I contract out the skip-chasing. The last time I had a full-time bounty hunter, he had the desk where you sit. See the gouge there, in your tabletop? He made that when he slammed a client's face into the desktop. Darn mean, but he sure liked working for me. I remember...."

Harry picked up his phone and stabbed the button for messages. He began to write down the times and the people in his phone log. All during this, with the phone cradled in his ear, he kept glancing up at Soulful. Soulful continued on, talked about the good times he and his bail enforcement agent had seen. After ten messages, three of them good for Harry and the rest hassles, Harry hung up. "Why doesn't this guy still work for you?"

"Got cancer and died. Smoked like a chimney. Not my fault, of course." Soulful beamed, sure of his virtue.

Harry decided to wiggle in something about himself. "I got some good news – one of the appliance stores I work with wants some radio spots, so I'll run down to see what their campaign would be. I'll be gone most of the day."

"Whoa there. Harry, I need the books closed for the half-month. That's our deal; you get a desk and a phone line for your own use, and I get the books balanced every two weeks. If you're gonna be gone all day, when will the books be closed?"

Harry rubbed the bald spot just at the top of his forehead. "It's okay, Soulful. The fifteenth is Friday, and the books will be finished Wednesday."

"Well all-rightee then. Back in the good old days, when I first got started, my receptionist was also my bookkeeper. Worked great. The good old days. A lot more crime back then, normal crime. Stolen cars, assault and battery, multiple DUIs. None of these brain-dead crack clients – naah, it was all pros. I opened my first office in '85 you know, and before that I worked for Big John Deleheney."

Harry rubbed his eyes with both hands. "I remember. You told me." He leaned back in his chair, stared up at the discolored ceiling. Maybe he was developing an allergy to linoleum.

"When I was a kid back in Missouri, I always thought I'd own a real estate company, or start an auto parts store or something. A living the family would approve of, a place of your own. Independence, self-sufficiency. I always knew I wanted to be a small businessman, even back in school, but I really lucked into my calling."

"How's that?" Harry massaged his temple. Streaks of light blipped around behind his closed eyelids.

"Why, the job with Deleheney was part time, to help make ends meet. But I took to it. The great thing about being a bail bondsman? You can always figure you're the nicest, most honest person in the room. Helps a guy's self esteem, you know. I couldn't tolerate your job – all those hoity-toity clients who think they're better than you. Being in advertising means sucking up, right?"

"Not that much. Mostly it's working with old friends who are also small businessmen, just like you. Why, most—"

"Maybe I should advertise. What do you think? A big billboard facing the courthouse? 'Soulful, The Lutheran Bail Bondsman. Money When You Need It.'"

Harry added, "Established 1985. For Your Family Needs. Albuquerque's Go-To Place for the Incarcerated. AAA Slammer Relief: A Business with Class."

"Yeah, 'Class.' I can get into that. Of course I get most of my customers by word of mouth. A couple of my friends work in the courthouse, and hand out my business card to those who, you know, are unfortunate enough to be on the other side of the bars."

Of course. Harry hunched forward over the desk, his head in his hands. "I thought most of your business would come from lawyers."

"Huh – lawyers. They got another agenda than me. All this plea-bargain horse manure? Speeds up the process. I want the time between the arrest and the sentencing to be as long as possible, so potential clients will get tired of that cell and want to walk the street in sweet freedom."

"A man's got to understand his business model."

"That's what my Dad always said. I remember him saying 'We Lutherans, we know how to be successes without being flashy.' He was a strict man."

"Like yourself." The smell of linoleum was making him a little queasy. He should have had breakfast.

"Bail bondsmen got a few simple rules. We live by them." Soulful's phone rang, and Harry ran for the door, leather briefcase in his hand. He had eluded Soulful's unending torrent of words.

Outside by the curb, his little Japanese car waited in its parking space. He no longer noticed the busted shock on the passenger side that caused the sedan to lean. Richard Martin had caused the sag, or so Harry told everyone in Rip's. He started the engine and flipped on the air conditioning – he wanted to drop the heat in this automotive oven before the sweat popped through his shirt.

———

GUNS. HALVARD'S AMERICAN FOUR-DOOR SQUATTED in a strip center, in front of a pawnshop. This pawnshop was up on Central near Louisiana. Certainly not the Martin pawnshop. Certainly not in his own neighborhood. Past the crucifix that hung on its chain from his rear view mirror, along with a pine tree deodorizer, he scanned the come-on signs taped to the inside of the shop windows.

We Buy Gold.

Gently Used Items For Sale.

Car Title Loans.

We Buy and Sell Firearms.

His palms sweated; his wrists itched under the edge of the starched cotton. He had to have a new one. A big one. A man-killer. He scratched at his baggy tan pants, tussled with the bulge, his *big* bulge.

It had been too hard this week, all of them pressing on him. Their hands clutching at his arm, their faces gazing up. All except his wife, watching him from across the room. Him plastering on his phony smile, his happy-face.

Just one more gun. He'd hide it in the garage with the ammo, up under the insulation.

———

By the time Harry finished with his client, he thought it a better plan to hit Rip's for Happy Hour rather than a liquid lunch. He drove down Lomas to talk to an actor friend of his, made some calls on his mobile from the car, and returned to the Bosque. Midway back up 6th street, he stopped in at a taco stand, got late lunch to go, and drove over to the soccer fields. This gave him a nice place to eat outside, and gave him time to think about his next financial deadline without interruptions from Soulful. He brought a circular blue pillow with him from the car, set it on a bench in the grandstands, and settled onto it with a protracted sigh. The grass smelled wet, like some place other than the desert.

The kids playing soccer appeared babyish to his eyes. They were all of the age where consummate skill meant making a pass to a teammate. Strategy meant running up and down the field in a squalling pack. Most of the soccer players dressed in the right sports clothes with expensive shoes, but one didn't.

The game broke up, and the players all ambled past the stands where Harry was ensconced. Some were towed away by parents from the stands, and some continued towards the parking lot where their grownups waited in their air-conditioned SUVs. The one in the dark bedraggled T-shirt lagged behind the crowd. Harry thought he knew the boy.

"Hey, GMR," he called.

The boy stopped down below him. His tee shirt didn't show soccer balls or goals or club names — instead it exhibited a faded logo of a motorcycle company and a dirt bike getting some air. Harry had been right, it was GMR.

Harry said, "You're kind of far away from your neighborhood, aren't you?"

The boy stared up. Not a word.

"I think you live a couple of miles away, down behind Rip's Bar, right? Whatcha doing down here?"

"Summer league. I play."

Harry could make out a darkness on the boy's face — heavy shadow caused by the sun overhead? With a little squinting though, he made out a large purple bruise covered the entire side of the face. "Where'd you get the shiner? Playing goal?"

"No. I dunno." The boy turned and started off.

"Want a ride? I'm headed that way."

"No," GMR said over his shoulder. He jogged off.

CHAPTER TEN

DRESSED IN A BRIGHT YELLOW shirt with the logo of an auto parts store over the pocket, 'Whit' Whittington roamed the aisles of Rip's package liquor section, inspected a bottle or two. He made a thing of blowing the dust off them. When he had his selection, he brought it up to Tenn's register and set them on the dark chipped wood. "I'll take these." Cheap tequila and a mixer.

Tenn rang them up. "That's $21.86."

"Say, you haven't seen my boy, have you?"

"Uh, boy?" Tenn glanced across the counter. Big shoulders. Long eyelashes, a crooked grin. Elvis hair.

"Yeah, we live behind you, on the next street over. My boy is nine, short for his age. Looks Mexican – has black hair." Whit scratched the side of his nose.

Tenn stared harder at the man. Blue circles under his eyes. "Well, we see more kids around the neighborhood in the summer. Your son – he missing?"

"No, he's just a funny kid, doesn't spend much time at home. I only wondered if you had seen him. Today." Whit rubbed at his nose again.

"'Fraid I can't help you. What's his name?"

"Gerald Whittington. And I'm Whit Whittington."

"Pleased to meet you, Whit. We'll keep an eye out."

Whit clutched his package, ducked his head and rubbed his nose again. "Thanks," he said, and headed for the door.

Tenn glanced across at his friend Richard. "That was interesting."

"You didn't tell him much." Richard swirled the White Russian in its glass and peered into it with one questioning eye.

"You didn't tell him anything." The neon over Tenn's head hummed louder, a little crescendo that surged up and died away, between ticks of the big bar clock. Maybe burning out.

"Not my place to inform." Richard turned to Julio the Adulterer, who occupied the next stool. "You know what that was about, what the story is?"

Julio said, "Sometimes I think I get a beer-and-wine license for my Taquería. Then I won't have to come in here and listen to you two gossip."

"Yeah, we're a couple of old women, aren't we?" Tenn turned to hang a glass up in the rack.

Richard wasn't ready to be waved off. "No, really, this isn't gossip. This is the study of family dynamics and the reaction of a neighborhood to that family, in toto. A tale of two generations, played out over the panoramic landscape of the alley behind Rip's. A saga of youth and lost childhood, of a rebellious child and his besotted father."

"Besotted father? No sé lo que eso signifique." Julio raised his eyebrows. "Dios, Tenn, give me the one minute version, so I don't have to listen to the half hour mi perseguidor would give me."

"Okay. Party house across the alley; mom and dad drink hard all the time. Out of the four kids, there's one who doesn't like living there. He sleeps rough. Bums food off of people, including you my friend."

"Oh, you mean that little Mexican kid in the dumpster? I don't

60

take much notice of him. We give him a taco or a burrito every once in a while, but that's it."

"Kid is named Gerald Matthew Roger Whittington, and most people call him GMR. That was his dad who was just in here, the Anglo."

"So?" asked Julio. "How come you didn't rat the boy out?"

Tenn paused. His face wiped itself blank. "That would be taking sides, now, wouldn't it?"

"And how about you, Señor Richard Martin. You didn't say nothin' to the daddy."

"I did take sides. I'm against parents, based on the good example set by mine. I'm also against children in general. Noisome little things, normally covered in messy substances and always needful of your attention. Vermin, really."

"Hoo hoo hoo, cabrón!" Julio said. "Very judgmental. And Tenn, he doesn't judge anything."

Richard said, "Our barkeep, he must be Swiss. He feeds the boy, but only sometimes, and he sells liquor to the father."

"Not often enough," said Tenn. "Dad doesn't come in a lot. They probably get their alcohol wholesale."

"But you got a family that's going to pieces on booze," said Julio. "And you're okay selling them tequila?"

"Not my place to make those decisions. Mr. Whittington is a grown-up. He makes his choices, and he'll buy a bottle here or elsewhere. You could even say a bottle's not *too* bad, because it's not drugs."

Richard concluded, ponderous, deep voiced, "Best that Rip's receives the profit. I desperately need this establishment to remain in business. That is the same reason that I patronize Julio's Taquería, my friend."

Julio laughed. "No, you come into my place because you're too lazy to walk more than a block. Pues, Julio's Taquería is very pleased to have your business."

ON THE NEXT STREET OVER, Whit did some business. He perched in a chair and hovered forward over the coffee table, as the Asian man on the couch leaned towards him. Whit wore ripped jeans and an open cotton shirt over a white Tee. He reached up to scratch at a hole in the T-shirt. Two glasses between them, ice gleaming and encrusted with bubbles, floated on wet rings. The Asian, Tommy, reached out with his finger and traced the scar of a cigarette burn on the tabletop.

Whit gazed at the bracelet hanging off Tommy's wrist, reflecting the golden tequila. "So you didn't come by the house for a drink then?"

The man grinned and fished in the front pocket of his slacks. "No." He threw a fold of money onto the table in front of Whit and leaned back. The visitor's eyelids dropped down, hidden.

Whit stared hungrily at Tommy's chunky diamond-embedded watch, fingered his own Seiko. He picked up his money, and leafed through it. "It's short a hundred."

"Count again."

He thumbed the bills, "One, two, – twenty – thirty. Oh." He shoved the fat bundle into his back pocket. "So what's next?"

"I need another new SUV. Something with all that gold trim and tinted windows. It's got to be black, with alloy wheels. Fully tricked out inside."

"You want gang or soccer-mom? Domestic or foreign?"

"German, if you can get it. More lawyer car than banger."

"When?"

"I ship south in four days. Got to have it by then to top up the load."

"Could be tough." Whit shook his head. "I don't have anything like your SUV coming into the auto store. I'd have to recon a few parking lots, scout around."

"It's a rich town." Tommy waved a hand. "I'll kick you another grand for this one."

"Thanks – it'll help."

"You'll have to find it quick."

"And find it in the right place. My ass needs to stay off camera. I'm leaving the parking garage at the hospital alone." His wife ambled into the room, her face drawn and older than her husband's. She showed off a melancholy expression tonight, but her tight top emphasized those pushed-up breasts.

"Intienda, babe. Look who's here. It's my friend, Tso Ban Nguyen."

The Asiatic grimaced as Whit mangled his name. He stood and offered the woman his hand. His beautiful white teeth flashed out in a smile, canines showing.

"Tommy Two-Win." She clutched his hand, cradled it. "We haven't seen you in a while."

"I brought you something." He handed her a bottle in a designer bag. "It's chilled, and I know how you like this one."

She accepted the bag from his soft hand, her fingers lingering a bit over his. She fished the bottle out from its colorful wrap, exposed the gold foil and black body. "Tommy, you're too good to me. I'll be right back – I think we still have a champagne flute." The two men watched her big buttocks sway out of the room, wrapped tight in black capris.

63

Tommy inclined his head towards the woman as she left. "She good with this car business?"

"Used to it, more like. You know how it is. They want you clean, but they also want those expensive shoes and phones for the kids. You got any kids, Tommy?"

"None that I know of, but not for lack of trying."

Whit snorted, leaned forward and tapped Tommy lightly on the arm with his fist. They heard a "paunk" sound from the kitchen, and Intienda sauntered back into the room with the bottle and a single glass. She poured and the foam soared up. Ducking her head quickly she slurped loud at the bubbles. The foam receded into the glass and she poured again. When it crept up into a golden dome at the edge she nestled her lips on the rim, threw her head back. The champagne disappeared.

"Good, Babe?" Whit watched her lips on the rim, her hand on the stem.

"Forget it, Whit," she answered. "This bottle is mine." She waved her finger at him and said, "Stick to those tequilas."

"By the way," he said. "Christmas comes early this year." He reached into his back pocket, and brought out Tommy's money. He inclined his head over the gift, handed it to her.

Intienda turned it over in her hand, considered its bulk. She tucked it into the top of her shirt. "Oo, muchacho, you know where to find it when you need some of this." Whit laughed. Tommy watched her, a smirk toying the edge of his mouth. She patted the top of her breast and gazed at the Asian.

———

THE WHITTINGTON HOUSE ROCKED. LAUGHTER and greetings filled up the house over the thump of the stereo. Two more friends named

Larry and Antoine arrived. Whit shook Antoine's hand, gave Larry a bear hug. "Great, man, glad you're here. Party time, Antoine. Make yourselves at home."

The two had dragged a young Latina woman along with them. The three dumped down on the couch and broke out cans of beer from their twenty-four-pack. The girl seemed to be half as old as Larry. Intienda loomed over her, hands on her hips. "I need to see some I.D., Miss, before we can serve you in here." The other four snickered and hooted. They loved the little routine.

"How old ju think I am?" asked the girl.

"Sixteen, seventeen."

"Naah, I'm eighteen. I'm legal."

"To screw maybe. Not to drink."

The girl flapped a hand. "Masticas mierda."

Whit nodded and grinned at Tommy. Two-Win, sprawled casual in a sagging chair, gave the impression he owned the room. Larry and Antoine continued on with a conversation that had arrived with them unfinished. Antoine leaned over past the face of the Latina, and said to Larry, "But you didn't tell me what happened next with the Weasel and your ten air conditioners."

"Where was I?"

"This fence had just showed up with two big guys in the alley."

"Oh, yeah. So I sez to him," continued Larry. "I sez, you come close to touching that, I kick your ass."

"Kick your ass," repeated Antoine.

"That's right, kick your ass."

"So then what did he do?"

"Oh, he puffed up like some toad, making big with his chest and his arms. He comes closer to me and...." Larry got distracted, and leaned over to nuzzle the Latina's neck.

"And then what?"

Larry's face rose back into view. "He says, 'We could have trouble over this, but I tell you what. I think trouble is bad for business. We gonna keep this one low key. I can be a reasonable man,' he says."

"What the shit does he mean, 'low key?' What does that mean?"

"It means he backs down, talking big all the time. He gives me ten C, a sniffer of coke, and takes half the load off my hands. He says he agrees not to screw with me no more, because I'm good for business." The two men cackled and the Latina stared past them, unfocused. The conversation wound on for a bit and she slumped back into the couch pouting. The screen on the back door slapped.

The Latina's chin popped up as Bud entered the room. She leaned forward, bunched those breasts outward and up with her upper arms. Bud showed for her too, throwing over a glance of bored indifference. "Seen GMR?" He asked his father, while he considered the girl, head cocked.

Intienda, sharp-eyed, didn't buy it. She waggled her fingers at the two. "No no! Not in my house with my son."

Bud, busy with his smug little grin, missed his father's reply. Whit prodded the boy, and repeated, "No, I haven't seen GMR. Have you?"

"Oh, yeah, down on one of the ditches to the River. Yesterday or the day before."

"Did he say anything? How'd he look?"

"He looked like GMR. You know, kind of snotty. All head-down mopey." Bud reached down between Larry's feet and got out a beer.

"He say anything?" Whit repeated.

"Nuthin'. So I grabbed him by the shirt, you know, by the shoulder. I figured he wuz about to run. I asked him where he'd been." Bud opened the beer.

"You should have asked him when he was coming home."

"I did that too. He didn't say anything. Just 'around,' and 'sometime.' So I smacked him one and told him to answer straight up."

"I wish you wouldn't hit GMR. It's not your place."

"Yeah, well, you wasn't there, or you woulda smacked him too. So he starts blubbering, then he twists out of my grip and takes off like a rabbit."

"Did you catch him?"

"Sorry. It was hot and I wasn't gonna chase him down. What would I done with him if I caught him? Drag him back?" He gulped, a slug from the can; foam startled up out of the top. He caught it with a slurp.

Whit shook his head. "It would have been a start. Then your mother and I coulda talked to him. You're the eldest – you need to be thinking about what's best for your brother and sisters."

"Yeah," said Bud. He wiped foam off his lip, rubbed his hand on the chair.

CHAPTER ELEVEN

Rip's had its big night on Saturday and its big season in summer. Tenn had all five tables full inside and three old men outside, parked on the brick planter that squatted in front of Rip's wall. He carried three cold longnecks, dangling them in his hand, and strode out to check on them.

"You boys doing okay?"

They measured it out. "Sure, Tenn, sure."

"Nice night, Tenn."

"Good sitting out in the cool. You should try it, qué no?"

Tenn held up the three beers, clanking together like bells. "Thought you might have finished your first round. Need another?"

"No sé." "Why not?" "Can't dance."

"Now, you boys know this is against the law."

"An unnatural law if you ask us."

"Anybody drives by, especially the police, and you make sure the bottles are on the ground behind your legs."

"Christ, Tenn, you think we're fifteen? I spent all my life hiding the bottle." Tenn choked back his laugh and ducked back inside to help Regina with the customers.

He swung the door open into the noise. Rip's had no live music except on Fridays and Saturdays, and only then because of a scratch band. The band formed up early in the evening, and played for themselves. They set up between the bar and the package liquor section. Julio's brother Amos brought in the guitar, a big flat top from Amos's mariachi days. He played it standing up, with the guitar riding high above his big belly. Cheezsy Brezinski played the accordion. Cheezsy, born Milo in Warsaw sixty-five years ago, hunkered down in a chair, hidden from view by the bellows of his instrument except for his wrinkled, dark face and his black scraggy hair. Susan McNally played spoons and sometimes made up nasal Appalachian songs to go along with the Polish Mexican Rancho-Grande Euro-polka. Tenn considered himself tone deaf, and therefore didn't care about the canned music he piped into Rip's – but he had a soft spot for the circus atmosphere his musicians brought. And he knew his patrons liked it. The music stomped and waltzed, clattered and fingered its way through three cultures. Of all the patrons, only two paid close attention – a pair of old, brown women solemnly danced in a small space in front of Amos.

Tenn crossed the room, checked on the tables as he marched through. Getting back to his counter, he hopped up on his walkway and spoke to Regina. "Big night."

"We got it under control. They're all locals, and they're coming up here rather than make us go out there."

Tenn nodded to the customer in front of Regina, beamed at her. "Hello, Rhonda. How are the kids?"

"My oldest, Jeffie, enrolled in college last week. Rebecca, my youngest, won an award for best essay in her grade. Ann, my middle, has become a real bitch and is the worst kind of teenager, and you don't really give a damn. But thanks for asking."

"Well, I admit I like children best when they come of age and can be my patrons."

Regina said, "Rhonda here is thinking about changing jobs."

"Really? I thought you had a career with the Post Office."

Regina laughed. "Men have careers. Women have a succession of heartbreaking jobs that go on forever but never go anywhere."

"You speak from experience?"

"I'm on my fourth job. Rhonda's had five."

"But the Post Office is a good gig, isn't it Rhonda?"

Rhonda said, "Reg'lar hours. Full benefits. But the scheming bastards are outsourcing the local station, and to stay as a federal employee, I have to go downtown to the Central Sorting Facility. Filing by zip all day every day – it'd drive me crazy..."

Tenn said, "Check with Albert Sanchez. He runs a furniture store down near Osha. He might be hiring."

"Thanks, Tenn. I'll call you if I quit."

He nodded and filtered down the bar. His sister Lavinia sat on a stool back from the counter, leaned against the shelves. She smelled of primrose. He nodded. "Lavinia."

"Tenn." They didn't have a lot to say. She knitted away at another one of those things that had no identity for him – until it suddenly emerged as a sweater for a baby or a woman's winter hat.

"Thanks for coming down to help."

"All hands to save the ship."

"Ah," he said. "Here comes Russell. Looks pretty drunk."

She stared at Tenn. "And how did that happen? No mind, I've got him." Lavinia hopped off the stool, left the knitting behind, and stepped to the front. "Russell, how's business?"

Russell was forty, short and soft, with manicured hands and helmet-like hair. He leaned on the bar, one shoulder dipped deep, and turned his face up to the thin, weather-beaten woman. His left eye closed and his right squinted up into wrinkles of self pity. "Oh, Lavinia, each day has barely enough cuts and perms to keep the doors open. Cut 'n Curl should be named Snip and Starve." He delivered these words without any slurring or hesitation.

Lavinia, amused, patted his hand, "I'm sure it will get better. Summer is slow in your business, but once there is something to dress up for, then the women will come in."

"Hit me again please, Lavinia." He betrayed his condition while nudging his glass forward – he tipped it over. It rang on the bar, rolled back and forth on its side as both of them inspected it.

Calm, silent, Lavinia uprighted the glass, swept the ice cubes in the sink, and used a bar towel to mop up the liquid. She got a new glass, filled it with ice, and poured water from a pitcher into it. Sliding it towards him, she said, "You're cut off, Russell."

He reared back from the bar, then leaned forward to stare at her with shock. "It's not like I gotta drive. I can walk home."

"Russell, you know I don't negotiate. You drink water for a while before you get another one."

He clasped the water glass and weaved back to his table. As he got there, he announced loudly, "Hey, Lavinia cut me off." The other people at the table jeered at him.

———

THE BAND WRAPPED UP ITS evening to scattered applause, and Cheezsy Brezinski was out the door like a scared cat, the accordion bagged up and hung over his shoulder. Amos and Susan both slipped up to the bar to lean against it, Susan parked in front of Regina and Amos in front of Tenn. Amos placed his order. "Can I have a Coke? And a bag of chips?"

71

"Sure, Amos. You guys sounded good tonight."

"Oh, it was okay. Cheezsy, he was playing theme songs from old TV shows. I hate it when he does that. Especially 'Bewitched.' Diablo, he has strange little ways."

"Well you made it sound good. More Monterey than Hollywood."

"Sí." The big man's eyes were cast down, his lower lip pendulous and grieving.

"What's wrong, Amos? I haven't seen you at any of the meetings lately."

"Oh, it's okay, Tenn. I been going to the ones over at the Presbyterian Church. I'm not drinking again."

"So what is it, big guy?"

"Pues, there's this woman who comes into the Taquería, knows me and always says hello. I keep thinking I should talk more to her, ask her out, qué no? But I also been thinking, what would she see in me? I'm middle-aged and fat. I work for my brother as a cook. I'm an ex-boozer who could start up again anytime. Not much to offer."

"Oh, hell, Amos. You got just as much to offer as any of us down here. That's why we're all here. There's something about each of us that keeps us on the bottom of the pond. This woman is in your restaurant. She's either going to understand or she's already one of us."

Amos smiled gentle, sad, and ripped open his bag of chips. "Thanks Tenn. You got a way to cheer a guy up. Good technique, telling me everybody here is big losers."

⸻

Susan, Regina, Lavinia, and Rhonda made up a foursome, shuffling the deck and snapping the cards down on the counter. The game was Slap, no skill and all chance. Regina led off with the card and the conversation. "Have you seen the dumpster boy lately? GMR?"

Rhonda shook her dyed-blonde hair. "Can't say that I have or haven't. He could be any of the kids who run loose during the summer."

"What do you mean?" Lavinia asked.

"Oh, T-shirt and shorts, sneakers, dirty."

Regina snorted. "Hiding in the corners. Eating whatever junk they want. Never coming when their Mommas call."

Rhonda agreed with the rant. "See, he's like any of our kids."

Lavinia pursed her mouth up, showing her age in the vertical wrinkles of her upper lip. "But he's always alone, and he doesn't wear the baggy shorts or have his thumbs on a phone texting."

Rhonda nodded. "Life must be simpler for GMR."

Lavinia said, "Simple, but not acceptable."

The cards dealt out, and dealt out again before Regina returned to her theme. "I've been feeding him." She arched her eyebrows, creasing her satin-black forehead.

The other three chorused, "Really?"

"Oh, yeah, we got a warm personal regard for each other. It's based on a mutual love of cheeseburgers."

"So how does this happen?" asked Lavinia.

"I bring his burger over to Rip's. He gets his lunch right before I get mine. We sit on the back step, and I watch him wolf it down in thirty seconds flat. I may have to splurge for two burgers, and kick in more fries. That boy has a hole where he should have a stomach."

"Could get expensive. Does he talk much?" Lavinia asked.

"Not much, but he's polite. Smells though."

"I hadn't thought of that," said Rhonda.

"Well, he's not going home to take a bath, is he?"

Susan scratched her spiky black hair. "Do ya know where he sleeps?"

"Not me," replied Regina. "Maybe we could track him by the smell."

Rhonda flipped out her last card. "Believe I take this hand."

Lavinia dashed off to open a beer for a customer, and when she returned, the cards had been shared out. The game began again. Susan said, "I can get him a shower. Y'all know I work dispatch for the big plumbing company?"

"Which one?" Lavinia asked.

"Ace Reilly and Sons. It's over aways, on Masthead."

"Do you like it?"

"As well as anything. But that's not why I brung it up. We got a locker room for the guys. With showers."

"No wonder in that," replied Regina. "A plumber can get into some nasty shit."

"There's even a ladies' shower. Of course, I'm the only girl there, and I just pee. I don't acsh'ly shower at work."

Regina flipped out her last card onto the pile, and cocked her head to the side. "Where you going with this, girlfriend?"

"Let's see if we can sneak the boy in and out, let him get cleaned up. He could lock himself in the ladies'."

Rhonda said, "More likely to sneak into a plumber's shop than to follow any of us into our homes."

"Well, that's true. He's a runner." Regina stuck a hand into her hair. "Tell you what." She nodded at Susan. "You come over here Tuesday at noon. I'll introduce you and you can make your pitch."

CHAPTER TWELVE

S ERENE, Tso Ban Nguyen gazed around a quiet charming restaurant in the mall, very Frenchified, that served high-priced slices of quiche. Out on Paseo del Norte, the mall was the type of Mexican that the Yankees liked, chi-chi but not quite right, with tiles made in China, plastic panels for walls between the stores, and skylights for a train station. Not the Bosque.

The tablecloth was starched and stark white; the waitress was pallid white and pierced through the eyebrow. She lurked against the wall.

"Come on, Tommy," said Intienda.

"You should try the Quiche Lorraine here. It's excellent." He lounged in his chair, sideways to the table, one diffident hand rotating a spoon in a circle, legs crossed casually, elegant loafers on display.

"Please?" She had a catch in her voice.

"But if you want to go all out, you can have the Eggs Benedict. On me." He waved his hand in the air over the menu.

"It's not eggs I want, and you know it." Her eyes darted away from his and locked on the floor.

"Yes, I know, but you have to play the game, now, don't you? We don't want Whit to know how we spent our lunch hour, do we?"

"That's not very friendly, Tommy."

"But don't you think we're friends? Close friends?"

Her head jerked up for a quick glance at his face. "Okay, I'll have the quiche thing you said."

Tommy raised his hand and the waitress appeared as if by teleportation at his elbow. She said, "Yes, Mr. Nooyen?"

He snickered as she got his name entirely wrong. "We'll have two Quiche Lorraine, and some sparkling water. It wouldn't be bad either if you could bring a couple of those little salads with the field greens."

"Yessir, I'll be right back with your waters." She holstered her pen and slid back towards the kitchen.

He smiled and patted Intienda's hand. "So, let's make some nice little talk. Pleasantries always help the digestion, don't you think?"

She tossed him one of those mutating stares, one that started with narrow eyes that then turned down sadly.

"Oh, I know, you're not feeling very well right now, a little despondent. But this will help take your mind off it."

"Just a quarter gram, Tommy, that's all I'm asking."

"You can have as much as you want, doll, as long as you have the money for it." Her gaze lay on the table in front of them; her face glum. "Tapped out again?"

"Whit is bringing you another SUV tomorrow. Then when you pay him, I can pay you."

He cradled her hand in his, gentle, considerate. "You know my rules, Intienda. No accounts, no tabs, no IOUs."

"Please, Tommy, cut me a break here. You know how hard it is for me to get through the day."

"When you're up you're up and when you're down it's the worst

76

form of hell, isn't it? Well," – he reached across with his second hand to trap hers, pinning it down. "There is our arrangement, you know. A quarter for a little personal favor."

She rushed into it. "Yes!" Her eyes flickered.

"Let's enjoy our time together. You can hit right after."

It was an elegant little lunch. He ate with leisure, indolence. She poked the quiche around on the plate with her fork and pretended interest in his conversation.

The waitress delivered coffee in solid little cups, with a superfluous handle on the side that could not have admitted even the smallest of fingers. Tommy paid with a credit card. He grasped Intienda's arm, leading her out into the mall, pinching the back of her arm. She flinched but did not shrug him off. Tommy steered her on.

She asked, "In your car again?"

"Oh, no. I thought something a little more exciting, a little more out in the open." He turned her to the right, down an institutional hallway and into the Men's Room.

"Please Tommy, not here." Two men washed their hands, watched her in the mirror as she and Tommy crossed behind. They raised their eyebrows at each other, cocked their heads. But they also dried their hands and sidled out.

He directed her to a stall in the middle, nudged her in and closed the door. "Open your blouse. That's nice, very nice. The bra unhooks in front too. So so tender. I do love you, you know." Edging around, he straddled the toilet and faced the door. For a full minute Tommy touched her, as his pupils dilated. Then with a caressing gesture, he draped his hand on her shoulder and pressed down. "I think it's going to be a lot easier if you're on your knees, don't you?"

"Anyone coming in can see my high heels, my hose!"

"Yes, I thought of that."

REGINA WAITED ON THE CONCRETE step of Rip's back door, feet planted in the dust. Sun pummeled her body, caused sweat beads to pop out on her midnight-black face. The dumpster near her didn't smell too bad, this early in the week. She could hear him as he slipped down the side of the alley, but she didn't turn her head.

GMR stood by her, but out of arm's reach. "Hey, Miss Regina."

She nodded to the fast food bag that waited two feet on the other side of her, leaning a bit to one side. "Lunch is parked over there. And here – " She held out a small plastic bottle of orange juice.

GMR edged past her, not too close, and collected the OJ on the way. He dropped to the cement on the far side of the bag and dug into it, in a hurry. "Thanks."

From where she sat, she detailed holes in his T-shirt, black knees below the shorts, hair that was matted and sticking out in back. "Don't mumble, boy. And don't eat the wrapper."

The boy laughed as he attacked the burger. "There are two here!"

"Well, you missed Sunday and Monday." They were quiet for a bit, then Regina said, "I believe in speaking plain. Do you?"

"I guess."

"Well, here it is, plain. You smell. In fact, you stink."

"Oh." He considered the allegation. "It's not my fault."

"I want you to meet someone. A friend of mine."

"Why?"

"She had an idea on how you could clean up. Her name is Susan."

"I don't know." He tucked his chin down and wouldn't meet her eyes.

"She doesn't work for the City, and she doesn't even know your folks. She's waiting inside, if you say yes."

He threw her a doubtful look. "You sure it's okay?"

"It's all right. Nothing changes, child. You still live where you want, go where you want. Listen to her for a minute, that's all. I'll even pay you to talk to her. I'll bring you french fries next time."

GMR considered. "All right."

"Well then, I'll get her." Regina rose and moved her skinny little thighs and midsize butt in the door.

In a moment Susan shuffled out, ruffling her spiky black hair with one hand. She let the screen door bang, and the boy flinched. She dumped down on the step and cleared her throat. "I'm Susan."

"Miss Regina says you're okay." He shot a glance at the young woman dressed in jeans and runners, a plaid man's shirt over a wife-beater.

"Pleased to mee'cha." Susan stuck her hand out to the boy, across the paper bag.

He scrunched up his face, stared at the hand.

She drew her hand back. "Okay, I get it. We don't shake hands."

"Miss Regina said you wanted to talk to me."

"Yes. I think I can get you a regular shower." The word "shower" sounded like "shar" but the boy understood, she could tell.

"She says I smell."

Susan sniffed. "Oh, yeah."

"I don't mind cleaning up."

"Well, that's a beginnin'."

"But I don't want – " He stopped. He scratched the bug bites on his arm.

"To get boxed in somewhere?"

He nodded. "My Dad is looking for me."

"Ain't no one here goin' to box you in. I'm sure this would be safe. See, I work at a plumbin' outfit and we have showers, because

79

plumbin' is dirty work. You could come check it out, see if you wanted to take a shower on a reg'lar basis."

She caught him glancing at her, saw his face relax. Safe, at least for the moment. He got out the second burger and devoured it.

Susan said, "It's Ace's, over on Masthead. You could go 'round back. If there are any white trucks parked there, then one of the plumbers is in the shop. That wouldn't be good. If they're all gone, then the guys are all out on calls, and that's good. Do you know where Ace Reilly's is?"

Around a mouth full of burger, "Uh huh."

"So you go in the back, through the rolled-up garage doors. You'd go to the left, and look for the Ladies' Restroom."

"The Ladies?"

"Much safer than the Men's. You can lock the door behind you, and there are towels and soap. If anything happens you don't like, I'll be out front to help."

"Sounds okay."

"Do you have extra clothes?"

"Yes."

"I could maybe wash 'em every once in a while. I'd dump 'em in with the guys' uniforms. You could pick it all up later."

"Maybe."

He stood up and moved two steps away. She didn't push. He half turned towards her. "Thank Miss Regina for me. For lunch." He took two steps, glanced over his shoulder. "See you."

"Ohhh Keee." Susan didn't know what his decision was, or would be.

"Maybe tomorrow." He shuffled off. His sneakers raised little clouds of dust as he dragged his feet.

CHAPTER THIRTEEN

L ATE AFTERNOON, THE TIME WHEN night workers and the swing
shift pretended to sleep, before they got up already tired and
started over. When Amos closed his eyes, he first saw the packed
sand as an inverted horizon that ran away from his vision, off down
the road towards safety. His brain ran the scene. The blue edge of
sky spun as he scrambled up to his feet, staggered over the dirt. He
gawped around for the thousandth time at the pieces of Hum-V
scattered over the ground, splayed out from where the blackened
dirt and the burning core of the truck lay. When he began to count
bodies, that's when he opened his eyes and gave up.

Amos lay stranded in his trailer, in the double bed, stranded in
memory, angry and sweating. With a grunt he heaved onto his side
and fished under the bed for the rifle. His hand found the AR-15,
cool, reassuring, lethal. He hoisted it up and rolled over with it,
cradling it against his chest and fat belly, curled up around it. He
sobbed, but without tears. Only the wheezing.

―――

CHEEZSY BREZINSKI WAS ALSO IN bed that afternoon. Swinging his
legs over the edge, he popped up and dragged on his pants. Ilene

McKennet reached over as she lay on her side, stroked his back. "Where are you going, Milo?"

"You know I hate doing it here at your place."

"Why? It's a sin in either place."

"Huh. Can't get caught at my apartment, can we? No chance there that your boy will walk in." He twisted away from her hand and fished his T-shirt off the floor.

"Maybe Donnie should know from us before he finds out for himself. Maybe I should tell him."

Cheezsy torqued full around to stare at her. His eyes glared out of the neck hole of his shirt, one arm in and one out. "Are you crazy? He's huge. He could squash me like a little Polish cockroach."

"Donnie is the gentlest man in Albuquerque."

"It's the quiet ones that burn down the ghetto."

"What? Ghetto? I don't get it."

"No reason to. No chance you would. You're not only Christian, you're Baptist. Kind of in the majority, unlike us Jews"

She pulled her mouth down, made a sad shape of her eyebrows. "Stay a bit. I can reheat some pot roast."

"Sounds good. But no," he slapped her on the mountain of her hip. "I gotta go, get back down to Schul. I gotta vacuum before Hebrew class. Call you later?"

She smiled, the white of her teeth breaking out like the sun from behind a cloud. "I'd like that." She pursed her mouth. "We need to talk, serious. Soon."

"About?"

"The future."

He laughed. "Ilene, Jews got no future. That's why we sew diamonds into our clothes." He jumped up to escape.

TENN AND LAVINIA WERE IN their best church clothes for this visit. Lavinia wore her new floral dress with the white collar and a white hat skewered to her pinned-up hair. Tenn wore cowboy boots, khaki slacks, and a pressed shirt with a bolo. Neither of them looked forward to seeing Mrs. Kyber, or sitting down close to death's bedside. But this was what friends did. They didn't bother to get out the old car – they trudged the four blocks. A way to delay the visit. A slow procession towards that visit, a reminder of their own time coming.

Roger Kyber met them at the door of the little stucco. He was stoop-shouldered, thin, and had bristling gray hair cut military style. "Lavinia, thanks for coming. Tenn."

They stepped into the hallway. "How is she?" Lavinia asked.

In the dimness they couldn't see into his deep-sunk eyes. "She fades in and out. The narcotics have her pretty goofy." Tenn and Lavinia headed down the hall; he stopped them. "No, they had to move her to the dining room – we couldn't fit the new bed into her room." They all turned into the dining room, its table and chairs swept away to allow the rising tide of the hospital bed, the bucket of ice chips, the bedpan.

Mrs. Kyber, once a big woman, now lay thin and bony in the crisp blue sheets. The flesh of her face, once so corpulent, hung in smooth folds. Where it was tight across her forehead and her cheek-bones, the skin was white, translucent. In the soft wattles of her cheeks and pendulous empty chins, the color was yellow and cara-melized from the fire raging inside. She smiled, gentle, vacant. Tenn gazed into her dark unfocused eyes. Little girl's eyes, almost pretty.

Tenn felt Lavinia hesitate in the door, glanced at her. Lavinia's face was tense, drawn. He stepped forward. "Mrs. Kyber, it's Tennyson Dortmund. You were great friends with my parents, Betty and Luther Dortmund – back in Texas. I wonder if you remember me?"

The old woman's eyes blinked, and she considered the man before her. "I remember Betty and Luther very clear. Your mother...." She inhaled and exhaled two gargling breaths, rattling them in and out. "My, she could dance."

"Daddy hated dancing more than taxes. Couldn't find his feet to save his life. My sister Lavinia is here. Remember her?" Lavinia stepped forward.

"Yes." She gazed solemn at Lavinia. "I recall you, child. You wore blue."

Roger said, "She always wanted you to marry one of her nephews, but it didn't work out."

Mrs. Kyber said, "You went off to the circus. A yellow elephant. I remember you."

Lavinia said, "That's very kind of you." Her voice cracked.

"So long ago. So long."

Roger bustled around the room, drug out a couple of chairs. "Sit down, sit down." The chairs made little shrieking sounds on the dining room floor as he scraped them across the wood.

Tenn said, "When I think back, I recollect two places where a body could dance. One was the Grange, where church people went, and the other was the pavilion down by the river. The pavilion served beer. Different crowd." His voice sounded rushed, unnatural to him.

Mrs. Kyber stared down at her hands. She flexed them and kneaded the knuckles of her left hand. "I – I don't think I ever went there. The preacher was against it. It was red, all red."

Tenn shot a glance at Roger. Red? "Lavinia and I were just little children back then. I think we liked the pavilion, not knowing any better."

"What place?" Mrs. Kyber asked.

"You know, the dance hall at the river," Lavinia answered. She was looking not at the woman in the bed, but at the venetian blinds – ivory, dusty in the window.

"Yes. They raised cattle there."

Roger glanced at Tenn and Lavinia. "Are you getting tired, Mother?"

"Who are these people, Roger?"

"They're some old friends who have come to visit, Mother. Why don't you lie back and close your eyes for a bit." He patted her hand and in reply, she sank back into the pillows and closed her eyes.

The three sat by the bed, quiet for a while. To fill the silence, Tenn said, "She doesn't seem in any pain." He hitched his chair back from the bed, turned it to face the other two.

"No, no, the drugs are keeping her from that. She's in the process of letting go, they tell me."

"Does she know you all the time?" Lavinia asked.

"Well, most of the time, but sometimes it's more like this. She'll tell me the dangdest things. She re-lives little moments. Sometimes it's a little embarrassing. A son shouldn't know everything about his mother."

"This must be very rough on you, Roger," said Lavinia.

His old eyes teared up, pink-rimmed, glistening. "I work through it day by day. The Hospice people say it's normal that the family gets a little numb. Also, the family doesn't really come to grips with it until the end. That's what they say."

Tenn dropped his hand onto Roger's shoulder, patted him twice.

"If there's anything we can do to help."

"No, I've got Hospice dropping by to help me see to her needs. It all comes down all at once, though. There are times I feel sorry for myself, sad to say."

"Comes down at once?"

"Yes. Three days ago, the same day Mother quit eating, I found out my shop is in the way of the new bridge."

Tenn jerked up straighter. "New bridge? Your shop?"

Roger stared at him. His eyebrows crawled up his forehead. "You haven't heard? They're going to condemn a major piece of the neighborhood. They want to build a new bridge to relieve the traffic on the Alameda bridge to the north. If they go ahead, they'll plow up half the neighborhood. The other half will be stranded behind on-and-off ramps."

"But I heard it was crossing downstream. At the Botanic Gardens."

"You need to watch more TV. It looks like it goes right through Rip's block."

Chapter Fourteen

In the mid-morning glare, GMR ambled down the alley, kicking a sun-baked dirt clod in front of him, catching it with the left foot, then the right, dribbling the clod between his feet for a few short yards, but soon over-running it. Turning to get it back into play, he kicked it hard back the way he had come, and whooped, "Yesss!" A half-dozen pieces pinwheeled away. Back on course, he worked down Ace's alley then froze like a perched bird at the edge of the parking area, hanging behind the corner post of a chain link fence. No trucks parked behind the building, only a half dozen cars against the far wall. The boy sidled down the fence line, peered in the open garage doors and stepped into the shade inside.

His head swiveled to the left and the right, tracking for boogey men, or plumbers. The place lay quiet, abandoned, so he slipped along the way he had been told and found two doors, opening the one with a female sign, slow, cautious. He wiggled inside, finding a barrel bolt up above his head on the door, sliding it to lock the door. The boy poked around for a bit, to map out the setup. His pace went from slow to hurried once the clothes were stripped off. He turned on the water and jumped in even though it began teeth-chatter cold, grabbing the soap with both hands and scrubbing himself with great energy – missing major patches, including his neck, a knee and both elbows. The shampoo. A bright orange color in a bottle covered with flowers. The boy sniffed it, suspicious, then washed his hair with the bar soap. Turning off the shower, he shook himself violently like a dog. With a towel waiting on the bench, he only half-dried himself in his rush, and hauled his dusty clothes on as quick as he could. After cracking open the door and listening, he slipped out of the bathroom and jogged towards the back door. As the boy got there, a white truck drove up, spraying gravel. His little brown arms pumping, he kicked into a sprint.

———

DURING THE NEIGHBORHOOD'S SIESTA, RICHARD lumbered back from lunch. He carried his second burrito in a piece of brown paper. Between storefronts a narrow dark space, claustrophobic and intriguing, ran back to the alley. A corridor left vacant by a vague lot line. The boy had wedged himself into the gap, back to one wall and feet on the other, six yards back. Richard peered back at him from his sidewalk vantage point. "Hello."

The boy glanced over at the fat man's legs. He gathered his own legs under him, popped up into a squat. " 'Lo" He shot a peek back towards the alley.

"I've got a 'burro' here from the Taquería."

The boy raised his eyes up as high as Richard's hand.

"Julio gave it to me. Said that if I saw you, it was for you."

"Mr. Julio sent it?"

"Yes, that's right. Here, you take it. I'm tired of carrying it around." Richard was still planted out on the sidewalk, a long stretch away from the boy. He held out the paper-wrapped burrito.

GMR straightened up and inched forward the few steps necessary to get the burro. In his hands it appeared huge. "Thanks."

"Thank Julio, not me. You're going to need something to wash that down with. You thirsty? My shop's next door – come in for a second and I'll see what I've got." Richard grinned when the boy followed him down the sidewalk. The first in the neighborhood to corral the kid. While Richard unlocked the door, GMR crowded up nearly to his elbow. The corner of Richard's mouth twitched up smug. Bragging rights. He tugged the door open and stepped inside, trailed by the boy.

GMR stood barely inside the front door as the fat man maneuvered around the counter and into the back. As still as the shop contents, GMR froze there until Richard trudged back in with an ice cube tray and two bottles. "I've got margarita mix and club soda. Take your pick." He dropped two ice cubes into the old wine glass with the chipped base, his working vodka-glass.

"Soda."

"This is club soda. There's a difference. Grownups like it." Richard poured out an inch and leaned over the counter, extended the glass. "Try it."

GMR advanced deep into the pawnshop and accepted the wine glass. He wrinkled his nose, but drank the club soda down.

Richard watched the boy shiver with revulsion. "Let's try the green mix, then." He plucked the glass back, added more ice, and filled it. "I want to keep that glass. It's very valuable. A family heirloom, in fact. You sit down there on the floor and eat, then give me the glass back."

⁓

COMING IN OUT OF A pounding late afternoon sun and blinded by dimness, Harry eased in through the pawnshop front door. He

89

stood in the doorway and waited for his pupils to open and his retinas to work. As they came back on line, they painted an emerging image of GMR, plonked down in the middle of the floor with a saxophone. Harry could hear the clicking and the stops, and a throaty wheeze.

Richard said, "I don't have a reed for it, or else the little urchin would be irritating me past all rational boundaries. You're just in time – take him away."

The boy spoke, "You want me to go away?"

Richard tempered his voice. "Well, not until four-thirty when I close. And you still have to put up the sax. Harry, what brings you to my establishment?"

"To get my watch back."

"Ah, indeed." Richard shambled over to the appropriate case and fished in it. He raised one finger while he searched, and intoned,

"When I do count the clock that tells the time,
And see the brave day sunk in soft sweet night
When I behold violet dusk in prime,
And hear the chimes all silvered white.
When lofty trees I see struck green with leaves
Then summer's eve is girded up in sheaves."

Harry screwed up his face in concentration. "Keats?"

"You always guess Keats. Shakespeare, Sonnet Eleven. Here it is." He brought out a large, gaudy watch, laid it on a square of velvet in front of Harry. "One official Harold Weissman possession *returned*, in *return* for three hundred dollars. Plus the agreed interest."

Harry handed the cash over. "Thanks, Richard. I always worry it will sell."

"To do that, I'd have to place it on consignment with a friend down on Central, Harry. No one can buy a watch like this in our neighborhood. Why, it costs more than most of our local cars."

"It was my dad's, you know. From a time when men could wear diamond studded watches and not be accused of – ," he shot a glance down at GMR on the floor. "You know. Being a fag."

GMR asked, "Who's a fag?"

Richard growled, "No one here, kid. Now keep quiet or I'll throw you out."

Harry wrinkled his mile-high forehead. "Would you really throw him out?"

"I was talking to you, my little aged advertiser."

Harry strapped on the watch and contemplated its gold, its scintillating stones, its sheer bulk. He tugged the edge of his cuff up over the watch. It stretched the sleeve tight. "The only problem with Dad's watch is that it frays up all my shirts. See, the cuff wears out right here."

He pointed, but Richard gazed down at the glistening dome of his head. "Were you close to your Dad?"

"I didn't think so at the time. I was for everything he was against. I even grew my hair out and wore my first ponytail just to drive him crazy."

"Hmm. I see you kept that part of your legacy also."

"Yeah, I spent a lot of time not being my Dad, so maybe we were close after all. We got along okay."

Richard reared back from the counter. "The concept of having a parent one actually gets along with – that's an idea I find improbable. What was he like?"

"Oh, big man. Spent a lot of time in the bar at the country club. Drove giant cars with red plush interiors. He was an outgoing guy, big laugh, big smile, big times. Of course, we lived in a dump to pay for all that."

Richard pursed up his lips. "Sounds like you understood him pretty well."

"Yeah, and maybe he understood me." Harry glanced down at GMR.

The boy flopped one key down on the sax and inspected the valves to see which closed.

Harry nodded. "Kids deserve that, I think."

"The boy is listening, you know. Ask him what kids deserve." GMR threw Richard a glance, went back to the sax.

Harry shook his head. "Foster home, maybe."

Richard stuck out his tongue and made a flatulent sound.

"I thought you'd say that."

Richard waggled his fat finger from Harry to GMR and back. "You two are a lot alike."

"Sez who?"

"Look at it from my perspective. You're both small."

"Everyone's small compared to you, Richard," Harry said.

"You both have poor hygiene and bad haircuts."

"I beg your pardon!"

"No need to get testy. You also have long and improbable names. Say, kid, what's your name again?" Richard asked.

GMR drew himself up, recited, "Gerald Matthew Roger Whittington."

"Well, Gerald Matthew Roger Whittington, meet Harold Llewellyn Weissman."

The boy jumped up, shook Harry's hand, and thumped back down on the floor. He picked the sax up and gave a throaty wheeze into it.

Richard said, "I always meant to ask you about the Llewellyn part of your name."

"Oh, they gave me the name of my dad's best friend. Lew was Welsh, and he and my dad did everything together. Looked like bookends, two giant guys in white shirts and loud ties, holding down a booth in their favorite bar."

"Getting named after a parent's friend is unusual. Normally it's for a grand-dad or something."

"So now you're an expert on Ashkenazi families?"

Richard huffed. "I am rather well read, you know."

"The real story is that my father married a Christian, so the family divorced him. That's how I got Lew's name. My Dad was kicking back on all things Jewish, like only getting names from dead people. And the irony?"

"Yah?"

"Mom raised me Jewish. More set on it than my father."

Richard released an exaggerated sigh. "How conventional. And here I thought your life was more interesting. It's four-twenty – let's close up early. I want to get over to Rip's before the meeting."

"Meeting?"

"Tennyson wants to talk to some of us in the neighborhood. Something about a coalition to oppose the bridge. Surprised you didn't get the word." Richard heaved himself off his stool. "Come on, GMR. Stash that sax back in the case. We're going to Rip's and I'll buy you a soda. A real soda."

As they left, Harry drooped his hand onto the boy's shoulder, just for a second, to see if the child could be touched. GMR skittered to the side, out of reach.

CHAPTER FIFTEEN

R EGINA LAY IN THE BATHTUB, steam rising up to the yellowed ceiling. Her eyelids blinked, trembled in surrender, eased shut.

Young again, she played in the yard. The fenced-in space had grass, but she preferred the dirt under the old sycamore. Hardpacked there; the ball could bounce and the jacks wouldn't be lost in the weedy dogtooth grass. Her momma occupied the rocker on the porch and shelled peas. Regina was surprised; Mother had white hair – her skin below it was wrinkled up, dark, dry. Her walker stood right by. "Momma," called Regina, but her mother gave no sign of hearing her, continued shelling, shelling. The peas dropped into a paper bag that said "Potato Barn." A hypnotic plunking.

Christmas time, but hot, very hot. Carols came from the radio in the house. Sweat dripped down Regina's side, soaked in at the top of her underwear. She knelt on her knees, reached out to get the scattered jacks. To start the pick-up on the first bounce, she leaned back, buttocks on her heels, then rocked forward. Her hand darted back and forth between the ball and the jacks. The ball moved in a line of vivid green, and the tree cast a red shade. It made her skin dark purple, luminous.

"Momma, am I late for school?" Regina shot a glance back at her mother and saw four children on the porch, all parked side by side in the glider. Four white children who murmured together. Mother said to the children, "Hush. You'll bother Regina. She has to study." Regina knew who they were: all her momma's miscarriages.

Her father drove up in the horse and buggy he used for special weddings. He halted the horse short of the yard, got out, and hung a weight on the lead rein. Striding around back of the buggy which had transformed into the bulbous family car, her father got his leather attaché out of the back seat.

"Regina." Daddy towered over her. Stood on a box, wore a white shirt and a black tie. "You should take more care when you're wearing a dress. The entire neighborhood can see that giant caboose of yours, flashing that white underwear. Looks like a full bed sheet, child." Daddy stepped down off his box and clumped into the house. He didn't even glance at Momma.

Regina knelt in Rip's. The bar empty – the earth floor packed, littered with peanut shells. The shells hid the jacks. The ball was a big scoop of white ice cream; it melted in her hand, dripping into the dirt.

RIP'S AIR CONDITIONING THUNDERED OVER the quiet desultory voices. Tenn had two tables jammed together. A few people gathered around, slouching in their chairs or leaning forward on their elbows. Soulful told a story about a felon to Harry and rolled an olive around in his empty martini glass. Julio had a beer in front of him. With slow methodical shakes he salted it, ignoring everyone else. A field of water rings both wet and dry stood out against the dark wood of the tabletops. Richard traced one with a finger and set his White Russian down centered upon it. A small tattered

95

book, binding loose, waited beside the lowball glass. Short lines left-justified ran down the pages, blocked into stanzas.

Tenn glanced at the book – Richard's eccentricity, as if he didn't have enough. Tenn leaned over to Lavinia and asked, "Who else is coming?"

"Reverend Halvard."

"Who?" asked Richard.

"The Baptist minister."

"You are jesting, Lavinia. In Rip's?"

"No joke, Richard. It's his neighborhood too. And my friend, Helen."

"Madame Librarian. We are well acquainted." His eyes circled the table. "Is this all? Shall we be so alone in our time of need?"

Lavinia blew her breath out. "Bob the Taxidermist is in civil court this afternoon, and today is Mr. Russell's busy day. Red Donnie might make it, but he said he'd be out Paseo del Norte re-keying a house first. Missus Chang would never close her bakery before seven p.m."

Tenn pointed at the door. "Here's Miss Helen now, with the Reverend." Helen Parch swept in and GMR's eyebrows shot up. She settled in beside him, bracketing him between the two women. He squirmed.

Tenn stood up and shook the Reverend's hand. "Dr. Halvard, I guess."

"Yes indeed. I don't believe many of you are in my flock. Can I get introductions?" They did the rounds, all but Halvard stiff and uncomfortable. The Reverend pointed his finger at GMR in a pistol gesture, mimed a shot, and winked. GMR, slumped down in his chair, glanced up at Lavinia.

Lavinia asked, "Did you bring it, Tennyson?"

"Here it is." Tenn dropped a newspaper on the table with a small three by five map surrounded by print. "Here's where the bridge will come across the Rio Grande."

They all got to their feet, leaned over the paper, and peered down like the Magi on the Child. Harry squinted at the map. "Even if I wasn't old and half blind, I couldn't make anything out from that."

GMR had been stranded on the outside, behind the towering backs of the adults. He cadged his way around the table and found an opening under Soulful's elbow, by Miss Parch. "What is that a map of?"

Miss Parch ruffled his hair with her hand, ignoring the jerk and duck of the boy. "It's more correct to say, 'What map is that?' or 'What does that map show?' 'Of' or 'to' should not be used to end a sentence."

GMR cast a solemn stare at Tenn. Tenn shrugged, and they both turned doleful eyes to Miss Parch. In her blue pantsuit, hair seized back in a knot, glasses black and rectangular, she appeared to be someone who might slap the backs of their hands.

Tenn told the boy, "The highway people and the City may build a bridge. It might come through here, but we don't know."

"Oh." GMR scrunched up his eyes, gnawed his lip. "Can I use your phone?"

Puzzled, Tenn handed him a flip phone.

"No, it has to have a real screen – yes, like that," as Lavinia handed him her smart phone. "How do you spell Albuquerque?"

Miss Parch inclined her head down to his ear and murmured, but he shrank back. "It's okay. It'll take ABQ."

Soulful waved a hand and said, "Let's assume the worst. You know, maybe the bridge comes through the back door. What can we do about it?"

Tenn cocked his head. "What do you want to do about it?"

"We got two choices. Move. Or move."

Richard said, "And where would we move to?" Shooting an alarmed glance at Helen, he said, "I mean, which location would you target for our move?"

Julio's mouth dropped, lower lip out. "Y que nos tienen? The old Albuquerque is going away. The Bosque is very la-di-da now, no? Everybody salvo nosotros, except us."

Lavinia added, "And how could we all go together? We can't move a neighborhood."

Soulful eased his glass towards Tenn. "All things change, you know, for bitter or sweet. I should probably move closer to the Courthouse anyway. This is a way for me to get out of my dump of an office with a bagful of state money. You can get out of this crappy old bar and make a boatload at the same time!" Tenn ignored the martini glass.

Harry said to Soulful, "Don't count on me going with you. My client base is here near the river and down in the industrial area."

GMR held the phone out to Tenn. "Here it is. A map. It shows where the new bridge comes through. There are some other lines."

Tenn accepted the phone, staring over it at the boy. GMR said, "You can zoom in and out, if you want."

Instead Tenn gazed deep into the screen and held it close to his eyes. "It's at the end of the block."

Richard hoisted both fat arms up in the air. "And what Rough Beast, its hour come round at last, slouches towards Bethlehem?"

Lavinia frowned. "Even we know that one, Richard."

He thumped a pudgy finger onto the tabletop. "The center will not hold."

Lavinia leaned her head close to Tenn's ear. "Rip won't like it."

While Tenn shook his head at Lavinia and made a shushing

sound, Harry shot his head around. "Rip? There's a human being named Rip?"

The old couple, the brother and sister, stared at Harry.

"Just ignore me then." Harry sank back, giving it up for the moment.

Tenn waved his hand in a circle at those around the table. "What if the center could hold?"

Julio asked, "Our strip center?"

—⁓—

HELEN PARCH DROVE THE FEW blocks to her Library and parked behind it in her reserved space, leaving her car paint to change its color and texture in the sun. The building waited, blonde brick stacked up cool, unemotional. Helen entered through the back door, through the staff room and the workroom, spotting new boxes that would need unpacking and cataloguing. She found her staffer at the reservations desk, checking books in. The young girl asked, "How did it go? Good meeting?" Her simple smile charmed.

"It went well. Have you been busy?"

"No, the usual. Several of our old dears have been in, checking out the latest mysteries and sob stories. I've got a couple of men using WiFi on their laptops and a woman who runs out every five minutes to jabber on her phone."

Helen contemplated her domain – the shelves that arrowed their convictions across the main room, the fluorescent lights over each aisle, the brown carpet that announced city aesthetics. Always a right word to fit in the right sentence, and here she had all the words. "What's your project for today?"

"I'm taking the 'fresher course' on collection management – part of my certification."

"That's good. Do you need to use the office?"

"No, I can do it up here on the desk PC." They heard the outer door bang open, and then the inner door swung wide. A child froze there. GMR's age. He gasped hard through his open mouth, his eyes wild, rolling. The boy darted past their desk and on back into the stacks.

A milling bunch of teenage boys boiled through the library doors, bringing in a tumult of shoving and loud, cracking voices. They hung up in the front of the library, checking it out. Helen said to her assistant, "Go find that boy and escort him to the staff room in back. Lock the door and call 911." The girl scurried away from the desk into the quiet of the library.

Helen Parch marched out from her desk, counting the boys. Seven, most smaller than her. Maybe they were fifteen-year-olds, a couple closer to eighteen. "Can I help you?" She kept her voice steady, all business.

They dressed much alike, in T-shirts, in banger pants, in baseball caps worn backwards and sideways. She thought they appeared unformed, soft, not yet baked. "Can I help you gentlemen?"

Uncertain, they flicked glances at each other. They had a clear leader though. Wore a black knit dome of a hat that hid his hair and forehead, wore a black T-shirt that depicted the Madonna in silver. White boy, nearly a man, not at all soft.

He thrust one of his pack to the left and another to the right. They sloped off to each side, to skulk past her at the greatest distance possible. The leader stepped towards her and tried for the distraction.

"No, come back here," she demanded of the two. "We'll talk first. What brings you in today?"

The leader surveyed the support behind him, then faced her. A disarming smile. "A friend of ours just came in. We tryin' to catch him up."

"And what's your friend's name?"

The little hesitation. "José."

"No José came in here. Now, gentlemen, I'm afraid before I let you in, I have to see your library cards."

"Yeah, right," she heard from the back.

They glanced back and forth at each other, shuffling their athletic shoes. "Or if you don't have library cards, then each of you should bring in a parent and fill out the forms to get one." The leader crowded up on her. Much bigger than her. "Should I be calling the police?" she asked them all, leaning past him.

The pack was melting away. Not the one in black though. He towered foursquare in front of her. Taking a step forward, he shoved his face down into hers, like a dog about to bite. Cigarette reek, and a smell of beer. A livid pimple, the beginnings of a beard. He shot out a finger like a stick and jabbed her in the collarbone. "My name is Bud. Remember it. If I want to fuck you up, there's nothin', nothin' the cops or you can do to stop it." He drew his head back, grinned a crooked smirk. "Have a nice day."

Defiant, he stopped to drink from the water cooler before he followed his troops out. His pants drooped down in back, showing plaid boxers and the crack in his ass. In a rewind of their entrance, the teenagers milled their way out the inner doors into the entry and paused there to swap some words. They jostled on through to the outside.

———

As the meeting commenced in Rip's, Red Donnie drove up Paseo del Norte, but not for a house call. The locksmith van carried him as far to the northeast as the road lay. He parked in his secret spot, snagged two bottles of water, and hiked up to the edge of the Sandia escarpment. There in the rockfall he could find refuge; up among the big boulders, there would be a space for him. A rock the size of a truck had slipped loose, leaving a split behind it with a little flat space. He climbed in, and waited for the chalky dust to settle. Dust motes floated down while his breathing from the climb calmed. A strenuous panting at first. Slower. Slow. The last of the powder made a film on his bare arms. He fished out the baggy with the mushrooms, chewed up three, and as the alkaloid taste filled his mouth, felt the gag of nausea. A slug of water from the bottle helped him get past the bitter tang.

As he squatted perfectly still, he could feel the beginning, the little insects running through his blood up from his belly, skittering into the back of his head. They moved on tiny velvet legs into the front of his brain, soothed out the headache that had lurked for days right behind his eyes. Then a wash across his mind, like a wave hitting the shore. The boulder that concealed him turned its shadow from a bluish gray to a dark purple, pinning that regal color to the ground below its own radiance. Thrumming on now, the trip was awake. He closed his eyes. Pyrotechnics flashed across the backs of his eyelids, gone crazy for a bit and then settled down into a wall of warm linen, fine woven. It barely held back the image of the sun. His heart, strong and content, pumped blood out from his core even to his toes and fingers so far away. He reached in and tugged out his consciousness from his eyes through his body, down those long

long arms, through the wrists and across the palms, out to the edges. He could feel his fingertips from the inside, and as his tactility flared so intensely, could feel the whorls of his fingerprints. Soon the gates between here and there would be opened, and the Messiah could approach through the linen sunlight.

It wasn't that he had to wait long, or that he waited short. Donnie hovered in a state that said, "not yet but soon." When the sun became fog, and the fog drifted down over him in the shadow of the cleft rock, he held his arms up and said, "Come again to be near me, and do not forsake me."

He did not hear the answer as much as experience it, as music, as pressure against his face, as a tinkling in his ear against his tympanum. "I would not forsake you, my child. We know each other well. Haven't we talked through all these many years?"

"I have come into the wilderness to be with my Savior."

"Yes."

Donnie let the presence of Jesus Christ flow down into him, so soothing and cool in the heat. "I don't find you in the city. I need you more."

"Yes."

"Time out of hand. Your time."

"Yes."

The dust cradled the shell of Donnie, the shadow of the rock held his consciousness. "How do I know, Lord, that this is real, that I am in the presence of You?"

"Trip after trip has brought us together, and still you have the smallest of doubt? I am your Savior and I am your path to God Almighty. We made the pact, in the flush of your youth. Walk righteously and I will always come to you."

Donnie held the promise, held it in his entire being. He became the promise.

"Now give yourself over to Heaven."

Donnie stood up and removed his clothes, twitching them into ornate, interwoven folds. He lay back down in the talc of the desert, and watched the photons of God splash into his skin, across his bony knees and radiant belly.

CHAPTER SIXTEEN

Bud crawled out of the window of the abandoned house, escorted by a thirty-year-old with a wispy fu manchu. Sunglasses hung on the grown man's forehead, held up by a do-rag. He said to the boy, "Saturday. We do it then. Ju first robo grandé, cholo."

The gangsta checked both ways up and down the street and ducked back in. The particle board that covered the window banged down behind him.

Bud wore a ripped black T-shirt, with a haloed Christ in white plastered across the back. His shorts sagged even more than normal, with a weight that bulged a back pocket. He had a small nine hanging there – his foray into gun-hood. He also had blood caked under his nose and a cut above a swelling eye. His lip was fat, his grin triumphant. Getting in had its expense, a price he had gladly paid. No more street rats. This was Gang. Family.

Bud strutted the street, on his way home. He had plenty of time. Now he had nothing to prove.

At the table they hadn't waited. Everyone ate Juanita's chili cheese mac as each preferred, either out of bowls or with the pasta wrapped in a flour tortilla. Intienda sat with Amy in her lap; Whit had the end of the table to himself. "Parts store was real busy today."

Intienda replied, "I thought you liked it that way."

"Oh sure, 'cause if the counter is slow I have to go into the back and stock."

"Any good opportunities?"

"There was a beauty of an old muscle car, a '69 Camaro. Shame Tommy Two-Win don't move any of them."

"Maybe we should get us a new car." She mopped Amy's chin.

"Something nice, but not too flashy. Don't want to attract attention. Not that you don't attract attention with that tush of yours." He grinned, a crooked zig-zag.

Intienda sponged orange cheese out of Amy's hair with her paper towel. Her hand shook, a slight tremor. "I swear, we have to get your hair cut, mija."

Juanita said, "I'd like to get my hair cut. In that new place. Something hot." She held up a limp strand of her hair.

Intienda shot back, "Dyed too, por qué no?" She frowned.

The girl considered. "Pink highlights?"

Whit laughed. "My little girl with hooker hair? Ain't gonna happen."

The screen door banged Bud on his heels, propelled him into the room. He ambled over to the stove and scooped some of the sticky mac from the pan to a styrofoam bowl and plunked down at the table. "Wha'zup?"

Whit peered at his son. "What's up yourself. You look pretty rough."

Bud lied smooth as silk. "I got into it with one of the jocks. But you should see him!"

Intienda narrowed her eyes. "So glad you could make it to dinner."

"Sorry." He wasn't.

"You know when we sit down to eat." She reached over and cuffed the back of Juanita's head. "I told you to put that phone up. Your friends can wait ten minutes."

Juanita dropped the phone into her lap, gleaming screen face-up, and threw a glance at Bud.

Bud growled at his mother, "Whyn't you leave her alone?"

Intienda stared hard.

He dropped his gaze to the mac and cheese, dug at it with a spoon. "She wasn't doin' nothin'."

"I decide what 'nothing' is."

Bud grinned. Let her think so. "Yes'um." He winked at Juanita.

Whit asked, ""How was summer school today?"

Bud glowered. "Like you care. But since you ask, school for dummies sucks. I'm gonna flunk English again, I think."

"Like father, like son. I flunked it twice myself." Whit leaned forward on his elbows, narrowed his eyes. "What's that on your neck?"

"Bandaid." Bud had a large patch that ran from his shirt up to his ear.

"You get cut?"

"Nah. It's a tattoo."

Whit grasped the edge of the bandage with thumb and forefinger, peeled it back to reveal a oozing terrain of bruise and red hemorrhage. "What's this going to be?"

"A fist on the end of an arm."

Intienda's voice burst out high, loud. "You little shit. That's gang, isn't it?"

"Naah, it's just something all my friends are all getting."

"Don't think we're stupid! You gone cholo, cabróncito!"

Whit jumped up. "I'll take care of it, Intienda. Bud, you and me – back yard. Right now!" The youth unfolded himself from the chair, slouched toward the screen door. As the screen slapped shut behind them, Intienda wriggled out from under Amy and rushed down the hall. Her door slammed.

Juanita patted the back of Amy's hand. "It's just us now. Mama's gonna sniff her way through this one. Dad'll get drunk. And Bud will be gone all night again."

Amy laughed, a low gurgling thing. She wagged her head at her sister and gazed up into her eyes. Amy's face was lit by the hot light bulb above shining down; Juanita's was shadowed under the glare, tipped down towards her sister.

BECAUSE THE BREEZE WAS RIGHT, GMR could pick out the river smell over the odors of the stable. The river lived out there close by, humid, soughing. He thought it smelled a bit oily and like rotting plants, but mostly the river gave off that aroma from after the rain. A scrubbed flow that wandered a distance he couldn't imagine, rubbing itself on the sand and the rock to become the cleanest thing he knew.

He crouched in the straw in the donkey's stall, down at the far end. The jenny ate out of a hay bunch hung on the wall, and her feet gave him room. Polite, she crowded over to one side. Dropping her head down, she belched grotesquely and made him laugh. Lying down beside him in the straw, she stretched out on her side, feet extended away from them. He leaned up against her back and imitated her long sigh. He could smell the straw all around them, and feel the stiffness of her hair. They closed their eyes.

EVEN IN HIS OFFICE, HALVARD had a couple of them hidden away, very close. He couldn't resist. Easing the laptop to the side, he reached down and tugged out the bottom desk drawer. Underneath a fat book, discourses on the early church. The Reverend reached in for one small bundle of cloth and then another. Unwrapping one, he revealed a black carry gun, tiny in his hand. The gun lay in his palm; the barrel and frame extended a bit past the end of his fingers. Halvard cupped the gun in his two hands, made it disappear. He brought both hands up to his chest, a gesture close to supplication, then bedded the gun in his lap. Nestled there, the pistol weighed down gently on his testicles and swelling penis.

The second bundle was larger. He dropped the rag and gripped the butt. Rosewood checked grips. Nickel finish. A three inch barrel. Dropping the cylinder out, he spun it and listened to the clicks in the quiet room. With affection he fingered the brass primers of the hollow points married into the gun.

CHAPTER SEVENTEEN

T ENN HATED THE MOMENT WHEN his eyes opened. An old feeling flared, a niggling anger that he had picked up in jail when sleep was the best way to pass the time. He didn't mind waking as much though if a dream had a hold on him. This time he dreamt he'd trudged out in the Yard, circling round and round the track. In the center all the muscle boys preened and sweated with their weights. The Mexicans occupied the bleachers. A small crowd in the corner, the corner of the weak. He avoided that space too. Hanging with the losers could get you cut up, robbed, butt-holed in the showers. Of course, he could talk to a guard anytime. If he wanted to end up dead.

Tenn strode the track every day – by himself, never choosing sides. He made himself as big as he could, marched head up and shoulders back. The left sleeve of his shirt was always rolled back, summer or winter, semaphoring the long white scar where he had been shanked – a scar that reminded everyone he didn't back down, and he wasn't easy to gut.

At first when the alarm clanged and his eyes shot open, he thought he was still inside. He expected to see the bunk above him, the webbing and the canvas, expected the regular striped light to fall across the wall at his elbow, the shadows of the bars. Instead, Lavinia's house, in the second bedroom. The ceiling shielded him, wavy with house-settling and re-plastering, banded with dark brown cornice. The pillow under his head was soft. Dressed in pajamas, not boxers and a T-shirt. A crisp blue sheet floated on top of him. The door wasn't locked.

―⁓―

EVEN IN LATE AUGUST THE morning was cool as Tenn drove to Rip's. Driving was unusual; normally he walked, but today he had an errand later. At the edge of his alley two cars passed by, a sixties family sedan that had been lowered down to a kiss away from the pavement and a hot blue jellybean of a coupe. He counted seven heads, all down low on the seat backs. The boys were coming home from work at the same time his workday commenced. Any day now the gang would be at his front door, crawling up into the neighborhood, changing it.

The first customer was the locksmith. Tenn set Red Donnie up with the shot and the beer. It was earlier than usual. Red Donnie jittered in place, jittered more than normal. As a response, Tenn leaned close across the bar, close enough where the waft of the whiskey in the shot glass bothered him, its siren song a need that filled his sinuses and struck through to muscle memory. "So, I'm going down to City Hall today."

Red Donnie said, "I haven't seen the boy around this week."

"Thought I would talk to our councilman."

"I worry, you know. I feel helpless. They could come by and scoop him up any time." Donnie sipped on the beer.

Tenn swept a bar rag back and forth on the shining, chipped surface. "I was going to ask the councilman about the bridge."

"School is soon. What will he do about school?" Donnie threw his whiskey back.

Tenn said, "There's also the people in Planning. I could check out what they have to say."

Donnie rolled the empty shot glass back and forth in his hands. "The school is bound to suss out his situation. Then that's torn it."

"They could give me an idea how likely the bridge is. How certain."

A deep swallow indicated the end of breakfast, the start of a locksmith's workday. Donnie belched discretely. "Where is he? Just dropped out of sight."

Tenn dismissed the worry with a flap of his hand. "It's okay, Donnie, he's around. GMR spends some time with Richard every day. Boy is a natural pawnbroker. Richard has him writing up the tickets, and GMR does a tally at the end of the day. He and Richard close the shop and then open Happy Hour here."

"We're all lost, with this bridge. The people behind it, they're unstoppable. More inevitable than war." The cadaverous man rotated back and forth on the bar stool, indecisive. The small man leaned on his elbows, watching his friend's anxiety manifest.

———

AFTER RED DONNIE LEFT, TENN found a marker and a sheet of paper and lettered up a sign. He hung, "Fishing at City Hall. Back at Noon" on the front door and took himself downtown to Broadway. Everything in the City offices was slick and shiny. '50s corridors stretched out in front of him, gleamed from polish. They maintained their own cool isolation from his strip, his neighborhood. He was glad he had worn a blazer. He wished for some litter, or at least dust, to waft up the hallways, to show some sign of the city's real life.

Tenn asked, "Could I see the councilman?"

Reception was Latina, as round as the moon, black shining hair and huge dark eyes. "Do you have an appointment?"

"No, but I'm one of his constituents. Wanted to talk about a neighborhood issue."

"Well, he normally talks to constituents on Fridays, but we'll see if we can fit you in. Here," she said, handing him a clipboard. "Fill out these forms."

"Forms?"

She tossed her long hair back. "Sure. It speeds things up."

"For who?"

"Us. Use the chair there. When you're done, bring them back to me."

—⁂—

TENN FILLED THE FORMS OUT and returned them. His receptionist beauty said, "Oh, good. Now the waiting room is just two doors down the hall on the right – you can't miss it. We'll come and get you if the Councilman frees up and can see you."

Tenn found the glass-circled room, rowed up with chairs like an airport lounge. He squinted at a misspelled sign that said "No Mobil Phone Use Please" and frowned at a TV that blared out a daytime talk show. The room already held eight people – slumped, fidgeting, stiffly erect, or painfully still. He chose a seat that faced the door, a hard plastic shell that pretended to be a chair. His feet barely touched the floor. For two minutes he tried to remain motionless while the aquamarine plastic dug into his hip bones. Tenn got up to sort through the magazines and chose one a year old, the cover wrinkled and stained but still intact. He returned to his chair and for five minutes flicked through the magazine. The only interesting article had been ripped out.

Inspecting his fellow detainees and being inspected by them used all of another five minutes. He may have been the most prosperous person there – hard to say. Three people, one after the other, gave up. Their faces were wrinkled up, creased with worry. Or maybe desperation. They faded away.

Dust, the dust he had hoped for in the hall, eddied out from the baseboards when the door opened and retreated back when it closed. A faint tinge of urine tainted the air.

After an hour, two women, two very young women popped in. Maybe thirteen-years-old, but possibly members of the waif-type gene pool. He was the last into the room, so he was the last talked to.

His waif introduced herself, "Hi, Mr. Dortmund? I'm Gloria Romero. I'm interning with the City Council this summer." Sharp chirping voice, high pitched.

"Call me Tenn."

"Yes, Mr. Dortmund. What is the nature of your visit to City Hall?"

"I wrote all that down."

"Yes, so you did. But tell me about it."

"I live and work down in the Bosque. We've seen the announcements in the paper about the new bridge across the Rio Grande."

"Yes, I've seen something about that too. Isn't it nice we can link the east and the west traffic like that!"

"Well, it might be nice unless it goes through your neighborhood. I wanted to find out where the bridge will come through, see how the Councilman felt about it."

She shook her head. "Oh, I wouldn't know what his position would be. I bet he likes it though."

"Can I talk to him?"

"I need to ask you some additional questions."

"Ooh-kay."

She leaned over to touch his knee and confide, "Now, you don't have to answer any of these if you don't want to. Federal and State guidelines protect you from revealing any of this that you consider private and personal. First off, what district do you reside in?"

"District two."

She checked a box. "Would you describe yourself as any of the following ethnic classes: Hispanic, Latino, Indian, Afro-American, Caucasian, Other?"

"Caucasian."

"Check. Would you describe yourself as a church-goer?"

"Yes."

Gloria ticked the box. "Occasionally, Often, Frequently, Weekly?"

"Weekly."

The pencil dug into the paper. "Are you Jewish, Moslem, Protestant, Roman Catholic, Other?"

"Catholic."

"Are you registered as a Republican or a Democrat?"

"Independent."

"Male, Female, or Transgender?"

"What do you think?"

She rushed through her rote summary. "Fine. That's very good. I've got you down as District Two Caucasian Roman Catholic Independent Male who attends church weekly is that right?"

"Yes."

"Now, have you ever attended a Council meeting or seen it live online?"

"No."

"Are you aware there is a master plan for the city?"

"I would hope so."

"You live in Albuquerque's Bosque, don't you?" She nodded, flared her eyes, and confided a secret. "Then your section of the city plan would be the Rio Grande Boulevard Master Plan. It's online."

"I don't have a computer."

"Well, you can bring it up on your phone."

"I have a cheap phone."

"Sorry. Well the Planning Office keeps one copy on paper for public inspection. They're not in this building."

"Figures."

She smiled. "Well is there anything else I can help you with, Mr. Dortmund?"

"Yes. I'd like to see the Councilor."

"Oh, that wouldn't be up to me; that would be up to his administrative assistant. You have a nice day, now."

———

TENN WANDERED BACK UP THE hall to the receptionist. "Is there any progress on me getting to see my Councilman?"

"He's very busy today. You do realize he represents one hundred and thirty thousand constituents?"

"Ah, but they're not here today. I am." Three people rushed out from behind the counter and clacked down the corridor. Two, clearly support staff, sailed in the wake of the third. Tenn inclined his head towards the three. "Let me guess."

"It looks like the Councilman is off to his noon meeting." Tenn spotted a large man in a brown suit as he scuttled down the hall, underlings clattering behind.

115

A SHINING MARBLE BAR TOP. Tenn hunched up on top of a stool, his feet hooked over a rung. A shot of amber fluid in front of him. He prodded it delicately back and forth with his index fingers. He considered.

Raising his hand, he signaled the barkeep. "Club soda please. And take this away."

CHAPTER EIGHTEEN

GMR HUNCHED UP IN A white plastic chair outside AAA Slammer Relief, swung his heels, front, back, front. He had his head tipped down and his hands folded in his lap. The man in the chair beside him leaned over the boy's head and conversed with the thatch of black hair. Sometimes he drawled along, and sometimes he spoke quick and intent. The boy answered. "Yes... No...Not much...Sometimes."

The man was bulky in the way hard work creates muscle mass. His skin shone a gleaming blue-black, his head was shaved. Scars, a lattice of white, ran down the outside of his arms and one cut his face from his earlobe to his eyebrow. He grasped the plastic arm of the boy's chair, dipped his head down to the boy's ear.

The door opened to the bondsman's office. It was Soulful, come out into the sunshine that pounded his sidewalk. "Hello boys. What's up?"

"Nuthin'," said the black man. The boy remained silent.

"Nice day."

"Hot," said the black.

"True. Nathan, I'm glad you hadn't already left. You forgot to sign the bottom of your brother's bond. A bond that big, I got to have the signature."

Nathan replied, "Pro'ly looks bigger to us than to you."

"Why don't you step inside and wait for me. I'll be right there."

Nathan got to his feet, crossed between the two, and trudged the three steps to the door. He swayed when he walked and his two huge thighs brushed together, bulged then loosened under the denim as he moved. The door closed.

Soulful squatted in front of the boy. "I see you met one of my customers."

"Uh huh. He likes football, not soccer. He has kids."

"Nathan's probably all right. Some of my other customers, though, they could be a little dangerous."

"Dangerous?"

"They might hurt people. They might hurt you."

"Oh."

Soulful reached forward and lifted the boy's chin, stared into his face. He placed his two hands on the boy's bare knees. "Promise me something. Don't talk to my customers. If you really want to, do it inside while I'm there."

"Uh huh."

"I'm serious. Let me hear you say it."

"I promise."

Soulful straightened up and found his phone in a front pocket. "Susan's looking for you. You remember Susan?"

"She works at the plumbers."

"That's right. She's been calling around, so let me phone her." Soulful selected a number out of his call log. "Susan? Soulful. I've got GMR here. Where are you?" He listened. "Sure, out in front of my office. He'll be waiting. Gotta go."

Soulful swiped his finger on the phone. The boy jumped up. "No no. Sit back down. Susan is at Rip's and she said she'd be right here. You willing to wait for her?" The boy nodded and popped back down in the chair. Soulful said, "Got a customer. See you around." The aluminum and glass door slapped shut behind him. In a moment, it opened again and Nathan lumbered back out on the sidewalk.

"You shoes all worn out. I can see your socks from here." He dug in his front pocket, tried to fit a book-sized hand into tight jeans. "Here, buy you some shoes." Nathan handed the boy a twenty and a ten. He rolled off down the sidewalk, made his way to a brown pickup with a blue front fender. As he got in, he checked back to get another look at the boy. He shook his head, backed out, drove away.

GMR had draped the money over his leg. He smoothed it, trued it up so the twenty hid the ten, peered down at the presidential portrait. Back bent, head down, he memorized Andrew Jackson.

———

SUSAN CIRCLED THE CHAIR ON the back step of Rip's, armed with scissors. GMR hunkered down into the chair, his shoulders wrapped up with a bartender's apron. The concrete held shards of hair, tufts and clumps of black. She said, "We should just leave all this here for the birds to make a nest outta."

"My neck itches."

"Wait a bit, we'll dust you off as soon as I'm through. How long's it been since you got your hair cut?"

"Maybe last spring. After school one day."

"Been a while. I din't really see any pattern that would indicate how it was cut. Hair normally tells a story, what it likes and where it's been. I been listenin' but haven't heard a word."

"Does hair talk?"

"No, it just leaves a message sometimes. Who cut your hair?"

"Mizz Russell."

"Mrs? Do you mean Mr. Russell?" The boy didn't answer. "That's a real good one. I can't wait to tell him he was mistaken for a woman." She snipped away, raised GMR's bangs up off his forehead.

"Will he be mad?"

"Naah, he'll laugh. People always think he's gay, but he's not. He's got a wife and a kid."

"What's gay?"

"Means someone who prefers to hang around with guys rather than with girls."

"Oh. You mean a faggot."

"Nasty word. Being gay don't mean you have to listen to words like that."

The boy soaked this in. "Do you know anyone who is gay?"

She snipped some more at the back of his ear. "Keep talking and I might cut your ear off, accidental-like. Hold still. Sure, I know a gay or two. Mr. Soulful, he's gay. I know because he and I like the same bar. Not Rip's, another one."

"Grownups drink a lot."

"Only when we can. Well, my work here is done. Ain't you fine lookin'." She whisked the apron off him. Hair launched out and up to float in the still heat of the afternoon.

CHAPTER NINETEEN

TENN HAD STACKED ALL OF the tables towards the front of Rip's and placed the chairs near the counter in back, lined up for the meeting. At four-thirty in the afternoon, he worried that no one besides his three – a large man drinking a White Russian, a Jew with a light beer, and a small boy with scruffled hair and a glass of milk – would show up. Somnolence hung thick in the room, muting Richard's voice, lulling Harry into a torpor.

By five Tenn thought Rip's wouldn't hold the crowd. Much to the chagrin of his afternoon drinkers, Tenn now closed the bar and wouldn't sell alcohol. A rising tide of people had washed in, driving the temperature and the sound up and up. At first it was restless movement, scuffling, droning – nearly a growl. It mounted as they came in. The room thundered and passions ratcheted up; the crowd practiced working out their indignation. Every row was packed, and a roaring careened across the room, echoed off the walls, and slammed back into a storm-center in the middle. In a cluster near Tenn at the front, five listening men bobbed their heads at a sixth, wise as judges. The sixth, purple in complexion and so angry spittle sprayed from his mouth, pounded a chair back with every point of his argument. The rest of the row held the silver-hairs. Four women

– three Hispañas and one black – shrieked back and forth to one another. Their voices rose like shrill birds above the room's baritone mayhem. The aisle up the middle was clogged with people who shuffled in a slow and tortuous mix, seeking seats, seeking friends, seeking God knew what. Only one corner was conspicuously quiet – a group of Latinos, men and women. They huddled close to each other, looking worried, shooting glances around the room. Tenn figured they wanted to be close to the back door.

He tapped Richard on the knee, nodded at them. "Our illegals. Ready to make a run for it if INS shows."

"What? I can't hear you. Are you sure I can't have another drink? What if I help myself in the store room?"

Tenn wagged a hand at him, dismissing him. He was dazed with surprise – not that his local patrons came out but that several business owners showed. And not just one but *two* churches. He called the meeting to order. "Hello, hello," he started. That didn't work. "Can I have your attention please." Only three people paid him any mind. He had no microphone.

Richard creaked to his feet, faced the crowd and did the fat man bellow. "Hey! Shaddap, will you! Tenn is trying to talk."

"Thanks Richard. I think." Tenn's voice shook a little, cramped with tightness in his throat. "Some of us locals have called this gathering to talk about the new bridge construction and how it might affect our neighborhood."

"You mean tear down the neighborhood," shouted a voice from the back.

"I'm sure you have seen all about it in the newspaper or on TV. They'll hold several hearings about this with the communities involved, and I believe we should be there united and ready to fight for our rights at those meetings."

A thin old man, bat-like and poised in his chair, shouted from the side, "What if some of us want the bridge?" His tone was querulous, impatient.

Tenn allowed, "Well, that's a valid feeling, too. Let's just go around the room and let everyone have their say about this. Why don't you lead off, sir, since you brought it up?"

"Who, me? I'm not for it. My house would either be torn down or end up in the shade of the bridge. And the drunks living under it would piss on my porch."

The crowd roiled like a wave. "Yeah, I would!" "Me too!" "Poor guy!" "Your house is shit anyway, Jorge!"

Tenn nodded, grave as a parson. "Okay, that's one of us who spoke his mind. Who wants to go next?"

Halvard, the minister from the Baptist Church, leapt up. The crowd, confronted with this tall heavy man dressed in black, dropped their chatter to a murmur. "I'll go next. You all know I'm a straight shooter, so I'll be honest and tell you the worst, straight up front. It looks like the bridge would cross over our boulevard here and dump out further to the west. An elevated six lanes, like Alameda. Now, it might go through our church, or further on down through Our Lady of Sorrows, but it will certainly blow away the block of buildings here. I would hate to see it go through the Catholic Church, even though that would cut down on the competition."

A few in the crowd chuckled.

Halvard nodded his head, beamed as if he had the crowd in his palm. He hooked his thumb in his belt. "And most Baptist ministers would welcome a new church, but I sense my congregation would prefer to stay right where we are. As far as coming through here, why, my wife has her hair cut close by, by Mr. Russell. I'm sure you all realize we can't have the shop where my wife gets her hair styled be torn down by outsiders. Coventry Cross Baptist promises to help in anyway it can."

Someone hollered from the back. "Save the Cut 'n Curl!"

Tenn held up one hand. "Thank you, Reverend. Who's next?" He chose Cheezsy Brezinski.

For two minutes Cheezsy harangued the crowd in a shrill voice, but they all got his repetitive point. "All change is bad. Once the Cossacks ride in, you gotta move every two years. If they don't butcher you."

Tenn unfolded his arms, cut the accordion player off. "Okay. Who's next?"

Rhonda got to her feet. "Hi everybody. My name is Rhonda, Rhonda Mayfax."

"Speak up! Speak up!" shouted several people in the crowd. And, "Where's Julio? Ain't he wit' chu?" Across the room, Julio ducked his head.

She rocked back, but sucked in a breath and continued in a rush. "I was born here in the Bosque and I've raised my kids here." Her voice trembled. "I recently quit my post office job so I could work in this neighborhood, and I'm still looking for a job close to home. I think the government's plan will cut our neighborhood up into four pieces, and I don't see how we could stand it. I think we ought to stop the project if we can." She slumped back down in her seat.

"Thank you Rhonda," said Tenn. The discussion slowed down, dragged on. Enthusiasm was overcome by anxiety, as most speakers worked through scenarios of loss. A smell – sweat, a melange of perfumes, the stink of cigarette smoke infused into clothes, the scent of fried food – hung over the crowd. People propped the doors open, shuffled their feet, scraped their chairs. Four witnessed *for* the bridge; others scratched their heads in indecision. People disappeared out of the back row – not many, but some. Not every-one wanted to speak, but probably enough.

At the end of the hour, Tenn summed up. "Well, the feeling I get from the people here is that most of us oppose the bridge and the River Parkway, and we want to be involved in any discussions held about it. I think people who are for the bridge should get their voices heard too, but maybe not here. Those of us who are against the bridge should do something about it."

A voice from the back asked, "What?"

Richard said, "Form a mutual protection league. Or a neighbor-hood association." Heads nodded all across the room.

Tenn said, "Let's adjourn this meeting then, and open one for those who want to band together. Those who want to participate should stay behind."

Nine people got up to leave. A man in a Hawaiian shirt and flip flops, sunglasses propped up on his forehead, said, "This's a pile of shit, and you know it, Tenn. We've already lost. We should just grab the City money and figure out how to use the bridge to our advantage."

A huge raspberry blurted out from the back of the room, along with a catcall. Tenn said, "I hope you're wrong, but you got to do what you think is right."

The nine left, dragging another two with them. The last guy out the door held his arm straight up, his index finger pointed to the ceiling. "Good luck, suckers!"

The room was now half-empty. A ripple of unease ran over the crowd, but Richard, fortified with a bottle in a paper bag, got them on track. "Okay, Tenn. What do we do first? Raise money? Go on TV? Get some leaders?"

The crowd murmured agreement, turned their eyes back on Tenn.

Richard stared up at him, his eyebrows scissored together. "Are you okay, Tenn? You look crimson, and your eyes are protruding. Is it apoplexy?"

Tenn shot him a scowl, then faced the crowd again. "Okay, how do we save the neighborhood?"

Within another half hour, they had their coalition, a name – the "Association Against the Bosque Bridge of Albuquerque" – and a list of things to do. Julio, vibrating like a wire, interrupted the feel-good complacency in the room. "My name is Julio Armenez and I own the Taquería here on this block. What I want to know is, who is going to run this organization? And I'd like to nominate Tenn." With a nod of satisfaction, he disappeared back into the crowd.

Tenn pushed down with his hands, shoving the idea away. "Uh, Julio, you can't have a bartender as your leader. Bad PR. Why don't we elect the Reverend here as our chairman, and I'll do some other job?"

By six thirty, they had a board elected and a next meeting scheduled – as the Reverend said, "Best we meet at the church."

Tenn said, "Well, that's one way to get me into a Baptist church." The crowd laughed. "Thank you, Reverend, especially for taking the chair."

The Reverend closed the meeting. Sotto voce, he said to Tenn, "Come early and we'll talk." His voice was shaky.

Tenn shot him a look in surprise. "Reverend, you okay?"

"Fine. Sure. I just thought, what if we don't pull this off? What if we let all these people down? The City does have us out-gunned, doesn't it?"

Tenn grinned lopsided. "Oh, we're not going to pull it off. We're doing this because it's right. We just have to try." He raised his voice to address the room. "The bar is now open." Just in time too, since

Cheezsy Brezinski had fetched his accordion and was pacing around wheezing out chromatic scales. Cheezsy found his stage space occupied by the Baptist Church, and the owner of the local thrift shop squatting in his favorite chair – he didn't like this. Terrier-like, he showed his incisors, scuttled into the aisles of the liquor store, and barked from a distance.

Half the room trickled towards the exit. The other half lined up at the counter. The clamor picked up, but it was bar-clamor, not politics. Friday night at Rip's was back in motion, and Cheezsy's accordion ripped and sawed through the noise of conviviality. Soon a guitar rang out, and clattering spoons added a beat like a milling machine.

—~~—

PLEASED TO BE IN RIP'S again, keeping an eye on the neighborhood, Lavinia hustled.

Helen Parch was enthroned at the bar, back straight, hands folded in front of her. She grimaced as other patrons occasionally bumped her, ordering drinks over her head. "Sometimes, Lavinia, I really wonder what you're doing in Rip's." She had let loose the tight knot of her dark hair, letting it hang onto her narrow shoulders. Her eyes were fishlike and blinking behind her magnifying glasses.

Lavinia washed beer glasses by hand. "Christ didn't spend his time only in the temple, Helen. He ministered to the thieves and the prostitutes." Unlike Helen, she wore no makeup, her skin dry and wrinkled with its seventy years.

"Looks like you're washing dishes, not ministering."

"And I could use some help, if you want to kick in about now."

Helen remained planted on her stool.

"Can I refresh that Coke for you?"

"No thanks. I'm fine."

Lavinia said, "I do like the way you pace yourself, Helen."

"No sense in losing control, Lavinia. I always keep my brain in charge." She stopped. Worse, she served up a portentous look to Lavinia. "Maybe it's the wrong time to talk about this, but I think you and Tenn should know."

"Know what?"

Helen asked, "Could you ask him to please step over?" Once she had her audience, she dropped her voice and made her two listeners lean forward. "There was a crew up near the Library today."

Tenn asked, "You mean a gang?"

"No, a survey crew. With compasses and poles and orange paint."

Tenn sucked on his lower lip. "Could have been the City. Utilities."

"No. The sign on the truck door said EnEmDOT. New Mexico Department of Transportation."

"Uh-oh. Highway Department," said Lavinia.

Helen nodded. "Yes, that is correct. I think we can all gather what that implies."

Tenn answered, "They're doing prep work even before the community meetings. They're in a rush, and we're screwed."

Lavinia slapped the back of Tenn's hand. "Tennyson! That word."

Tenn wandered off, muttering.

Helen said, "He didn't take that very well."

"He doesn't like being corrected by his big sister."

"Yes, I can see that might chafe." Helen leaned forward again. "So does he know you've adopted another foreign child?"

Lavinia said, "We all have secrets. Even you, Helen."

Helen widened her eyes, goggled them. She glanced right, left. "You haven't told anyone, have you?"

"No, of course not. I promised."

"It would be better if you forgot."

Lavinia wrinkled up her seventy year old mouth. "You can trust me. Unless I ever hear of you touching a child in your charge."

—⁂—

Some afternoons, if Lavinia had worked in Rip's the night before, she would nod off in her chair. TV didn't cause this problem – Lavinia didn't allow herself television during the day, only in the evenings. As was proper. Sleep often trapped her when she opened up one of her spiritual books, rueful though it made her. Even ones that weren't just religious pep talks, but demanded more of you. She thought that books should be demanding. Life should be ordered and strict, and each Christian should seek to become better. But even her favorite author Thomas Merton knew how short you could fall. She re-read *Ascent to Truth*. In her weakness, she dozed and dreamed.

Afternoon dreams were always cluttered and jumpy. Her children and Harcourt – her old beau – ran this dream. She waited at the church door dressed in white. He wasn't coming. Beside her, three children rowed up in their Easter best. Even little Michael had a clean face, clean ears, and a barely misbehaving cowlick. Lavinia's mother mounted the steps, hymnal in her hand. "I'm sorry baby," she said. "Without Harcourt, you can't have children."

Lavinia fled into the church, calling, "Harcourt! Harcourt!" Hysteria mounted up in her chest, choked her throat.

She was a teenager again. Her mother followed her, dragging Lavinia's three children behind her. "I'm so sorry, little Lavinia."

Her mother caught her by the wrist and whirled her around. "No husband, no kids." Lavinia's babies had disappeared. The church aisle broadened out into the parking lot. She searched for Harcourt's old jalopy. "It's okay," her mother comforted her. "We'll get you another beau. In the meantime, you can become Aunt. You'll make a good Aunt. Always there to babysit."

Lavinia tried to cry out and woke herself up. Thomas Merton tumbled to the floor. A fall that bent over several pages, dog-eared them badly. Mother could always be such a pain. Besides, Harcourt had never proposed. Time had made her, she thought, first the maiden aunt and then the sister who took in the family's problems. The family's babysitter.

CHAPTER TWENTY

TENN SAW REGINA'S ANGER FLARE red, burn hot behind her dark cheekbones: he slowed as he approached her. Parked at a table in Rip's, she stabbed at a baked potato with a mean and vengeful fork. "I'm going to kill him. The little shit."

Tenn, nonplussed, asked, "Who, the boy?"

"No, his sadistic brother."

"Because?"

"GMR is all black and blue today. He's got a limp. Bastard probably knocked him down and kicked him."

"Oh. Very bad."

"Can you loan me a gun, Tenn?"

"I'm sure Amos could, but are you sure that's the right path forward?"

She raised a lip, showing off a canine. "Gimme another diet Coke."

"You mean Rum and Coke. You're an angry drunk, Regina."

"Only today." She dug at the potato. "So what do you suggest?"

Tenn answered, "What I've always suggested. Get him off the street."

"No cops. No social workers."

Tenn rolled up his lip like a curtain and made a sucking sound on his incisor. "Yeah, I got you. Even if you women would let me make the call, Richard would never stand for it. My idea was to hide GMR away. With us, in plain sight."

"What do you mean 'hide away?'"

"Keep him off the street, keep him with one of us all the time."

Regina pursed her mouth. "So, afternoons with Richard. And Happy Hour here. What about mornings?"

Tenn held his hands out like he welcomed a congregation. "We get him a job at the Taquería. Amos spends early mornings doing prep work for the breakfast burrito crowd and then for the lunch mob. He can show GMR how to use a knife. Stand him up on a box, and let him chop onion and tomato."

"Hey, that's good, Tenn, even if it sounds a little dangerous. Would the boy like the work?"

"Who knows? He doesn't talk much more now than he did three months ago. You think you know him, but all you really know is he eats your hamburgers."

"Of course we know him. You are the biggest wet blanket in the Bosque, Tenn."

"And proud of it."

They both fell quiet. A fly droned by. Tenn armed himself with the fly swatter. The yellow sticky strips weren't working.

When Regina's potato had disappeared, she returned to the challenge. "What about at night?"

"I've got an idea." He fell silent.

"Care to share?"

"No, I think I'll ask the boy first. Maybe I can catch him tomorrow. Fair warning though – it's fifty-fifty he won't bite."

TENN CHECKED OUT THE BAR'S screen door to find GMR already waiting for Regina in the alley. He came out himself into the knife-edge sun and plonked down on the step, three arms-lengths from the boy. "Nice day."

Nothing.

"Do you like being out at night?" Tenn inclined his head towards GMR.

"No." The boy hunched over, his forearms on his knees.

Tenn made a mental note: time for Susan to cut GMR's hair again. "I can see you might not. There are other people out at night. Some of them might not be good people."

"You mean bangers. Or dopers."

Tenn checked out the cut lip, the bruising. "You know a lot about dopers, GMR?"

"Mom and Dad drink. Alcohol is dope too."

"I suppose it is."

"Those people over in that house," – the boy pointed off to the west – "They smoke a drug. They act crazy, and you never know what they'll do. They steal things at night."

"So living on the street isn't all that great. Let me show you something." Tenn started up the long flight of stairs at the back of Rip's. GMR watched him from the stoop. Tenn stopped halfway. "Well, come on then."

GMR followed at a distance. When they got to the top, Tenn stooped down and flipped back a mat to reveal a key. He jerked open the warped, sticking screen door and unlocked the wooden door. "This is the apartment that comes with the bar. We don't use it. I thought you might like it."

They stepped into a living room that lead to a kitchen. They poked around. A thick layer of dust lay like sheets on the furniture, and fly-specks spotted the windows. Watermarks overwrote the ceiling and each other, Rorschachs without symmetry. In the kitchen, an old porcelain sink with its chips and rust stains. The door of the refrigerator hung open with a rag stuffed over the hinge. The boy wandered back into a narrow hall and ducked his head into the bathroom and the bedroom. Tenn followed GMR back to find the boy seated on the sagging bed.

GMR stared up at him. "This is nice."

Tenn cleared his throat. "Here's the deal. You can use the apartment, but you have to clean the place, and keep it clean. You can have the key, but tomorrow Red Donnie can cut us another one."

"So I can live here?"

"There's one other catch. School begins in three weeks. You have to enroll. I'll go down with you and we'll do the paperwork."

"School is great. The rules don't change every day. Can I go with Miss Lavinia instead?"

—⁓—

REGINA PLANTED HER SOLID LITTLE feet in the alley's dust. She wondered what kept the boy. While she thought, her hand opened one of the bags and fished out a burger. Opening the foil she bit into the edge of the bread and began to chew slowly. Shouts filtered down the alley. Regina drifted towards the sound. Two voices. A few houses down she stopped to listen. A woman and a girl, angry with each other. The voices were strident, tearing along in Spanish. Regina stepped up on a pile of abandoned lumber, raised her head over the cinderblock wall. She recognized GMR's house. She watched.

CHAPTER TWENTY-ONE

L AZY WITH SLEEP, SUSAN LAY in her foldout bed in her apartment, naked under a crisp, newly laundered sheet. She heard clattering in the kitchen – a spoon in the sink. "Mary Beth, you better be making coffee, or I'll have to kill you."

"Relax, sweetheart. I've got what it takes to perk you up." Mary Beth appeared in the door wrapped in a giant robe – mid-fifties, stylishly gray, plump in the soft way that said "mother" or "grand-mother." Coming over to the bed, she handed over a cup of coffee and perched on the edge. "You've got a nice place here."

"Gimme a break. This apartment's a shoe-box with two posters on the wall. An' those are posters of the UNM Lobos."

"It's small, I agree, but you've done good things here." She touched the back of Susan's hand.

Susan yawned, made an elaborate production of sitting up and sipping on the coffee. "Thanks. Nothin' like your place, though."

"Could be your place, too."

"Not yet, Mary Beth." Susan blew across the coffee, floating steam across the bed. "I got sumthin' to prove first."

"That you don't need me?"

"That I don't need your money."

"More important to you than to me, sweetie."

Susan tipped her head to the side. "Um...."

"What?"

"Mary Beth, you're – you're so safe. There's nothing wild about you. I want to be dangerous, at least once in my life."

"Are your friends dangerous? That's the surest way to get down that road."

"Yes. No. Some." She ruffled her short hair.

"And I'll meet them tonight."

Susan shimmied into her panties, and struggled into a pair of jeans that were too tight. "If you want, sure. But first let's get lunch and do a museum. You're on vacation; you should be forced to swallow a little culture."

"I've got a better idea. Let's go to that good wine bar down on Central near the old movie house. We'll hang out all afternoon and solve this wildness thing." Mary Beth dropped her robe to the floor, moved like a cruise liner across the room, drew on a linen blouse with belled sleeves. "Have you seen my skirt?"

Susan rushed up behind her, encircled her with her arms and rested her chin on the older woman's shoulder. "I lied before. None of my friends are really dangerous. We're mostly just sad."

———

"THANK YOU FOR MEETING WITH US." The Reverend's voice spooled out smooth and pleasant as he addressed the three men.

"No problem. Always glad to meet with a community organization." Benjamin Taylor, Councilman for District Two, wore business casual. His button-down shirt was starched, his blazer was blue, his belt buckle Western. "I bumped into Trev here on the way out the door. He's Assistant Deputy Counsel for the City – I hope you don't mind that I brought him along." A feel-good smile plastered his round moon face.

Trev had the basic lawyer look – the suit and tie, wire-frame glasses. He set a leather briefcase on the table. "What is your association called again?"

Tenn handed over a business card, black ink on cheap white stock. "Association Against the Bosque Bridge of Albuquerque – AABBA."

Trev opened up the briefcase and extracted a leather notebook. He snapped the locks closed on the case. "So, you're on the board of AABBA? Are you a charity? A 501.C3 organization?"

The Reverend answered, "Already looking for problems, sir? No, we're not a charity, because then we would be prohibited from lobbying, wouldn't we? Welcome to my little church, gentlemen. I think you met Mr. Dortmund on the way in. My other fellow-officer is Bob Dobbel." The Reverend nodded towards the taxidermist.

Taylor replied, "Let me introduce you to my other colleague." Taylor indicated a man in a blue suit. "This is Carmel Torridon. He's with DOT on the construction side." At six-foot-three, Torridon towered over the others. His hair had been buzz-cut, and his sunburn half-hid a mass of broken veins threaded through his cheeks.

Murmured greetings and handshakes around the table; Taylor took the lead. "What can we do for you gentlemen?"

Bob leapt forward. "I'd like you to move your bridge so it don't come in my back door."

The Reverend chose words more politic. "What Mr. Dobbel means to say is we represent a group of citizens concerned with a major traffic change in our neighborhood."

"Personally, I see this bridge as a great thing for the City and the County." replied Taylor, as he leaned back. Now he owned it. "It's a definite step ahead, a real win for the City. The two sides of the River need a much better connection. If I had more say and more money, I'd build two bridges."

Tenn raised both hands out towards the Councilor and shrugged. "We're not against progress. We only want to limit the negative impact. Particularly for the people we represent."

Taylor gazed up at the wall above Tenn's head. His voice droned. "We assure you that in situations like this, we try to balance the impact on individuals with the greater good for the full community. Prior to announcing the changes to the Rio Grande Boulevard Master Plan, the City, the County, and the State spent much time studying the demographics and the financial impacts and gains of several options. I assure you we've done all due diligence."

Bob looked at Tenn and rolled his eyes. "Right."

Taylor went on. "I feel a rational inspection of the proposal will bear up under scrutiny. Your neighborhood problem is, well, problematic. Wherever we plant a bridge will impact a few people in a neighborhood – with most but not all results being desirable. Meanwhile the bridge will be a real shot in the arm for the rest of Albuquerque. I fully sympathize with your feelings and I wish we could help you through the transition. But at the end of the day, we represent all one million people in the greater Albuquerque area." Taylor paused for a breath.

The Reverend tried a smile, lips tight against each other. "That's a very thoughtful answer, Councilman Taylor."

"Thank you. We're thoughtful people down at City Hall."

Bob turned a bit pink. "I wonder how much thought you gave to jamming the bridge through at the Botanic Gardens?"

"Now, Mr. Dobbel, the Gardens are a large asset to Albuquerque."

"And we're not?"

Trev removed his glasses and set them neatly onto the gleaming leather of his briefcase. "You've of course thought about the compensation we pay? We do buy you out."

Halvard shook his head. "That's not an olive branch, that's a gun held to our heads. Fifty percent of the people down here are renters. Eminent Domain and the payments won't help them."

Taylor beamed, "So as renters, relocation is easy!"

Dobbel puffed up, about to explode. He came half out of his seat, his mouth open and his eyes wide. Halvard grabbed him by the sleeve, jerked him back.

Tenn rushed forward. "Mr. Torridon, you haven't said much. What is your take on all this?"

Torridon had been flipping his way through a stack of documents in front of him, signing and jotting margin notations. He flicked his eyes back to the meeting, grimaced. "My job's construction. I lay the roadbed where I'm told. Ben and Trev dragged me to this meeting to answer questions about how long things would be disrupted, how much it costs, how many companies and jobs that I will provide work for. I don't do policy, I do civil engineering."

Tenn countered. "Then tell us what you can do to minimize impact if the bridge goes through. Can you bury the ends of the bridge and the ramps? Can you make the bridge look good? Can you cut the traffic noise down?"

Torridon shoved the collection of paper to the side, leaned forward on his elbows. "I'm impressed, Mr. Dortmund. You've given this some thought. Well, if this was frickin' Washington D. C. and we had their money, we could do some of what you ask. I can promise the bridge will look like a slab from the sides and a freeway from the top – that's what any concrete pour can do for you. As far as the fancy buried off-ramps you're asking for, that's beyond current funding. Noise abatement, now that's expensive too. We *will* paint her titty-pink and hang turquoise guardrails on her – that's the only money for tarting her up we got in the budget."

The Reverend pursed his lips, "All this is a bit of a problem for us. As a matter of fact, nothing you have said would address any of our community concerns."

Taylor tried to smooth out the message. "Fortunately there are a number of community hearings coming up. Your voice can be heard at those."

Reverend Halvard flushed. He squirmed in his seat.

Tenn shot the Reverend a glance. Tears appeared to be welling up in the man's eyes. Tenn directed attention back to the Councilman, to give Halvard a moment. "So we can't influence the bridge location?"

"Not in any practical way," Taylor said.

"And we can't ask for upgrades that reduce the neighborhood impact?"

Taylor shook his head. Mockery teased at the corner of his mouth.

Tenn leaned forward, as close to Taylor as he could get. His whole face painted up an appeal. "And there aren't any offsetting programs or development the City would provide to save the neighborhood?"

Taylor said, "I've always trusted vibrant and dynamic neighborhoods to do what is best for themselves. Let the market take care of it. That's my philosophy."

"You know we will mount a campaign in the press," pointed out Tenn.

"Your prerogative."

The Reverend got back into the game. "And it's likely to turn political. We're not helpless here. We'll cast the issue as 'City Hall oppresses the poor and takes the side of the rich.' You are placing the bridge where you think the least influence resides and where the fewest votes can come back to haunt you."

Taylor rubbed his hand back and forth on the table-top, staring at it. His voice tolled out. "I'm sorry to hear you speak so harshly, Reverend."

Halvard said, "We have the moral high ground here and the press will see it that way."

The three men on the other side of the table eyed each other. Two leaned back and the third folded his hands. His nails looked like manicured claws. "Well," said the Assistant Deputy Counsel, "Mr. Dortmund here is a bartender whose establishment has been fined in the past for serving minors – and where ex-felons and people on bail have been known to drink. He might not be the caliber of person most organizations choose for their board. And Mr. Dobbel is not only a taxidermist but has also been cited by the City Health Department for processing game meat under unsanitary conditions, without proper registration and inspection. I think, Reverend, it will be difficult for AABBA to take the moral high-ground."

Taylor basked in the moment, folded his hands across his belly and beamed at the Reverend. Halvard was speechless.

Torridon shoved back from the table. "I think we're done here. I've got to meet with my engineers in a half hour. Let us know if DOT can help you in any way or can answer any further questions."

Taylor simpered. "Have a good day."

The three strode out and down the hall, two of them already thumbing mobile phones. Tenn turned to his compatriots. "What just happened here?"

Bob Dobbel slumped in his chair at the table, his head in his hands. "We are so screwed."

THE TAXIDERMIST, HIS FACE COLLAPSED into lines of discontent and as gray as fog, popped the trunk of his car. The tarp lay in folds as he had left it. He twitched one corner back, saw the delicate nose of the doe, the dark staring eye now clouded with death. With a continuous litany of grunts, Bob Dobbel forced his arms under the deer and the tarp below, got her up in his arms, and staggered in the back door of his taxidermy shop. Once there, he gutted the animal and poured her entrails into a large trashcan. Using knives and a saw, he roughly quartered her and stacked her inside a refrigerator without shelves.

Returning to his car, he stared down into the trunk. A quart of blood had seeped from his tarp and congealed on the nappy pad that lined the space. A sigh like a deflating beach ball escaped him. This had happened before: he knew what to do. He dropped a garden hose into the trunk, turned the bib full on, and ran water for five minutes. The water ran out through his rusty fenders onto the ground, at first the clotted chocolate color and then the brick-red, then the rose tints that only hinted of life. He turned off the hose and threw it up against the back wall.

He banged the trunk shut, dropped into the driver's seat, and slammed the door. Twisting the key, Bob made the old V8 roar and, staring behind him, shifted into first gear. Jamming the accelerator down, he leapt forward rather than back, peering hard the wrong direction. The car smashed into a dumpster and the left headlight disintegrated, folding its chrome eyebrow down into the front of the fender. "Shit! Goddamn! Shit shit shit!" He jammed the transmission into reverse and hurtled backwards into next door's concrete steps. The chrome bumper folded down, almost to the ground. The impact snapped his head back. He shrieked, a

142

wordless howl of rage, jammed the car into drive, floored it, and sprang forward twisting the steering wheel. His mangled left fender caught the dumpster, rocketed it out into the alley with the car, and guided the rusty green trash bin down the auto's side. As it came even with Bob himself, the dumpster ripped off the side view mirror and shattered the rolled-up window. Bob kept going.

Careening down the alley, he gripped the wheel so hard it should have fractured. His screaming rose to a higher pitch, "Bastards, Bastards, Bastards!" The power pole stopped the car dead, threw him out across the hood, and rather gently draped its wires down across the car, across the dirt alley, across the triumphant dumpster.

IN THE LATE AFTERNOON LIGHT of summer, four empties stood in a row on the step beside the Reverend. Regina handed him another beer, maneuvered around between his broad back and the screen door, and plunked down beside him on the concrete. "How's it going, Reverend?"

"Been better. Have we met?"

"No. I know your wife though. I can't help but notice you aren't inside with the rest of us."

Halvard flicked a glance her way. He said, "No need for a ghost at the table. I think I'll hide out back here and enjoy my little sin."

Regina waved a hand at a fly. They listened to the fly, to a mess of flies, all wild sound droning around the dumpster. She cleared her throat. "You act like a man bothered by something."

"Oh, you know." He flapped a hand.

"No, I don't."

"I'm going to lose my church."

"Not necessarily."

"They're going to drive the bridge right through the parking lot on their way over to I-25. They'll plant the off-ramp to Rio Grande Boulevard right through the sanctuary."

"It's just a building, not the Church itself."

"You don't understand the situation. We can't move. First, there's not enough money, even with the City pay-out. And second, if we move too far, I'll lose the flock."

"Ministers have had to move on in the past. Churches have closed. You can fight your way through this."

"Not much of a fighter." Unsteady, he leaned over towards her, peered at her shoulder. "You see. I lost two other churches. The first one, they didn't renew my contract. The second church asked me to leave right away, when a child got one of my shotguns at the parsonage and blew a hole in the front door. The Board wouldn't stand up for me."

"Rough break." Guns? She wasn't too keen on that.

"When we first interviewed here, I saw that the people – they wouldn't ask too much. They didn't expect any better than what they got. My wife and I have been here ten years. I thought it would be forever." He hung his head.

"Focus on the congregation, Reverend."

He ignored that. "I've been happy here, even if my wife hoped for more. Easy to project the right image, even if you're not on the way up. Even if you've lost the way so bad you get ineblierated ... uh, drunk on the back step of a seedy bar. Don't tell my wife, by the way. There would be hell to pay. It's bad enough I can't get it up, and now I'm drunk on beer."

"What?"

"Nothing." He held the bottle up to his mouth and she heard the click of the rim on his front teeth. Halvard drew hard.

"We'll find a lot close by and raise some money. You can start with a temporary building."

Halvard stared at her right in the eyes. "You joining my flock, Miz Talmadge?"

"Who, me? I was raised *Free Will* Baptist. That ain't gonna change."

CHAPTER TWENTY-TWO

MID MORNING IN THE LIBRARY. Helen leaned against a bookcase, gazing across the room, out of control. The rational part of the mind could not avert the eyes, could not command. Those eyes caressed the boy. She adjusted her glasses, reset the dark frames where they had slipped down a shiny nose.

GMR sat at a table in the library, a field mouse in the tightening vision of a hawk. Page by page, lingering, he turned his way through the book of pictures. One caught his eye, a pen and ink drawing. He opened up another book, to the back endpaper. Taking out a short gnawed pencil, he tried to duplicate the drawing. He had to erase often. Smearing the page, he pivoted from one big volume to the other.

Her breath drew shallow and hurried. Hands twitched, acting out a touch to the boy's hair. A moan hummed out through clamped lips. Too beautiful, the moan said. This was her agony.

GMR grew bored with his effort and closed the second book on his rendering. He eased his chair back on the hard carpet, just enough to wiggle out from under the table, and headed off to the men's restroom. She lingered outside that restroom. A pale, soft hand moved on the door, moved back and forth, traced out the grain. Stubby fingers, no rings.

Juanita lay on the couch, ear buds jacked into her pink phone and screwed into her ears. Her foot traced back and forth and a bar or two of tuneless melody snuck out of her mouth. Reflections from moving windshields on the street flickered in through the Venetian blinds and painted the ceiling. On the floor, Amy lay on her stomach and colored in a book with crayons and pencils. The little girl had built a ring of beer cans close by. Her toys. Juanita drifted off in sleep.

Amy dropped the crayon and rolled over on her side. Her face flushed and she curled up. When the fit kicked in, it jerked her over onto her back. Saliva bubbled out of her mouth, mixed with blood where she had bitten a lip and her tongue. Her eyes rolled back until only the whites showed and her head flailed from side to side. Her heels drummed the floor.

Intienda, asleep at the kitchen table, jolted awake at the drumroll of the girl's seizure. She lurched to her feet, and caroming off the walls, ran down the hall. Dropping to her knees she skidded across the living room floor and grabbed up her daughter. Intienda forced Amy's mouth open and inserted a spoon handle to keep her tongue from crawling back.

Waking late to the crisis, Juanita wrapped up in a ball against the couch back away from Intienda, who clasped Amy to her chest, pinning her down. The fit lasted a full agonizing minute. Amy came to with some residual twitching as her eyes tried hard to focus, shivering in their sockets. Intienda held the girl close. Juanita shrank back further.

Intienda, fueled on adrenalin and Kahlua, hauled herself and the girl up using the arm of the couch. She nestled Amy into a chair where the girl made little mewling noises. Intienda jerked Juanita up out of the couch by her arm. "I said watch her. You bitch. You worthless vaca gorda."

Juanita said nothing; she sagged in her mother's grip as if only that claw-like hand supported her.

Intienda slapped her slow and sure, front handed, back handed. "Bitch. Bitch. Bitch. Bitch." Each blow. One two three four. A pause while the mother got her breath. The hand jerked up into the air once again. It struck the girl's face. Five six seven. Intienda hurled her down into the nest of cans and turned back to her beloved Amy.

With a choked-off sound, Juanita began the long cry. She stumbled up to her feet, scattering the cans, and ran to the bathroom. The door slammed, shuddering in a cadence against the frame. A blood smear showed on the doorframe.

CHAPTER TWENTY-THREE

Rip's lay languid at four in the afternoon. Bright light came in the long rectangle of a window in front, making the dust motes glow against the dimness. Up at the bar, the neon and two hanging lamps made a pool of light and a little space for the three, the only three in the bar.

Two women lined up against one man. Harry parked his elbows on the bar, suspicious, and made an A-shape of his arms and clasped hands. His teeth chewed on one knuckle. It didn't help that he was on the stool that wobbled. "And to what do I owe this free beer?"

"Tenn put us up to it. We need you to step up for the AABBA," said Regina.

"Ask Richard."

"Richard can't do what we want," said Lavinia.

"And what is that?"

Regina said, "We need people all over town to take our side. We need an ad campaign. We need you to make it happen."

Lavinia reached forward and touched the back of his hand. "Do it for the neighborhood. Do it for Rip's."

"Okay. Anything for Rip's. And free beer. What's my budget?"

"We need it cheap," they chorused.

"A klog iz mir! Don't you people have any respect for professionalism?"

Lavinia started to speak, but stopped. She crossed her matchstick arms.

He drummed his fingers on the bar. He poked a bar mat back and forth. He sipped at the beer "Okay, I have a couple of friends who are ultra-liberal. They would do anything against 'The Machine.' I can get their voices for free."

"That's good. That's real good," said Regina.

"I can write the spots. Maybe I can come up with a theme and build up a package."

"That's even better," said Lavinia.

"But I have to pay the radio stations."

"Oh," they said in unison.

"I figure ten grand."

Regina said, "Ten thousand? Dollars?"

He grunted, "Uh-huh."

Lavinia slapped a hand down on the bar. "Might as well be twenty thousand!" She stared off into the far corner.

He shifted from one buttock to another, making the stool rock. "I could do a lot with twenty. But in the spirit of making-do, there are some freebies. Public radio and campus radio will carry it as a human-interest story. We might get an editorial or two. And I could maybe use the Internet. My daughter and her friends would be willing to blog and post on social sites."

"Your daughter?" Regina's eyebrows knitted together and she leaned in to be close for the answer. "What daughter?"

He stared down at his empty beer glass. "Some other time, Regina. Don't ask me to talk about my marriage and my daughter if you want a favor. A big favor."

Lavinia touched Regina on the arm in warning, then smoothed back to the problem at hand. "Ten thousand is a lot."

He snorted. "Not hardly. Are you still living in the fifties?"

"Okay," Lavinia conceded. "We'll ask AABBA what they can raise. I'll talk to Soulful. He never spends money except on flashy clothes. We'll ask around."

"What about Tenn?" he asked.

Lavinia snorted. "You're confusing him with Rip. Tenn doesn't have any money."

"Rip doesn't exist. At least that's the story Tenn puts out. Is that true?"

Lavinia finished the conversation by turning away to draw another beer. "Wouldn't you like to know. Just think of Rip as the silent owner."

He grunted. "We'll find out, sooner or later." He finished his bar nuts, scooted the bowl forward for another. "Well, if I'm doing my part, you all better be doing yours."

Regina said, "Don't worry. Red Donnie and I are working the petition drive. Soulful is looking for legal help. Tenn is holding a fund raiser here on Monday and Julio is bringing tacos. Only Bob Dobbel is out of the loop."

"Huh?"

"The Reverend asked him to step down. He's so angry, he wants to take matters into his own hands."

He asked, "How so?"

"Bob was talking about moving all the survey markers. He wanted to sneak sugar into gas tanks, slash tires. Tenn and the Reverend, they don't want anything illegal."

He tilted his head. "Maybe as a last ditch effort." The three heard the screen door slam and turned their eyes to the back.

Down the liquor aisle Richard lumbered, with GMR leading the way. Harry hauled out the bar stool beside him and slapped the seat. "Jump up here, GMR."

Richard waved a princely hand at Lavinia. "Please, dear friend, decant that remedy into mine glass, as rapid as the wind." He claimed a stool two over from Harry, wedging GMR between the two men. "Harry. I'm surprised to see you installed here so early."

"Richard." Harry dipped his head. "Feeling sarcastic today are we?" Harry leaned down to the boy's ear and asked, "Want some bar nuts?"

The boy said, "I have a job now. I'm a sous-chef. That means I 'cut veg.'"

"Well then, if you have a job you should buy me chips. Or peanuts."

Richard sighed. "Keep your hands out of the boy's pockets, Harry."

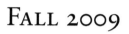

FALL 2009

CHAPTER TWENTY-FOUR

L AVINIA PLANTED HER FEET ON the doormat and knocked. The
door was flung open immediately. "Come," she said. "It's
time." She held the screen door open.

"Yes ma'am." GMR clumped across the threshold. He closed the
door, and with intense focus, locked the deadbolt. He thrust the key
deep into his front pocket.

"Let me see your neck." He bent his head forward, obedient.
"And behind your ears. Good, you got the worst of it off."

"Yes ma'am. Are we walking?"

"No, it's too far for an old woman like me. We'll take Tenn's car.
You can drive."

"Can I really?"

GRADE SCHOOL SMELLED OF WAX, an odor that steamed up from
the polished concrete where it lay exposed to the sun under the
windows. Lavinia and GMR hesitated in the double doors. She
clutched her purse and checked the manila folder one more time.
Cafeteria tables rowed up across the front hall of the school. GMR
tugged at her hand. "This way."

They found the table labeled "S-Z" and waited in line behind frustrated parents and bored children. When they got to the front, Lavinia announced in a grand tone, "Gerald Whittington, fifth grade." Her voice didn't wobble.

The aide, a motherly type with a PTA badge, glanced up at them and then hunched over the old PC on the table. Typing and peering filled up a moment. "Fine, I see him here. And you are? We're only allowed to complete enrollment if the child is accompanied by a parent or guardian." She goggled at them over her half glasses, twitched a strand of gray hair back behind her ear.

Lavinia said, "I called ahead. Grandparents are also allowed." She tried a conciliatory smile.

"Oh. Okay. Can I see some I.D.?" Lavinia presented her driver's license and the aide turned once again to her computer. "Your name isn't Whittington."

"I think you'll see that I'm in there as the maternal grandmother." She picked up on the look of incomprehension. "The mother of the mother."

"But there's nothing about you in the boy's record. It does say that his mother has listed her race as Hispanic."

"Yes, my daughter was adopted. Is there a problem?" Lavinia smiled, tight, intimidating. She was getting into it.

"Well, I think we can continue as long as one of the parents calls in and adds you to the file. Now, I need some proof that Gerald here resides in our school district."

"I brought a utility bill, like I was instructed on the phone." Lavinia handed over a piece of paper, a xerox of a bill that she and Miss Parch had altered with some difficulty.

"This is a copy. Do you have an original?"

"That's all the boy's father gave me."

"Well, I guess it will be all right." The aide handed the paper back, peering into the computer screen, her shoulders hunched up and her neck stretched forward. "No outstanding fees or fines from last year, except for a five dollar locker fee."

Lavinia dug in her huge handbag and came up with the five. GMR scuffed his feet. He began fiddling with one of the cables on the back of the PC. "Don't touch that," said Lavinia.

He jerked his hand back. "Yes'm."

"We'll be placing him in Mrs. Elvis's section. You'll get a chance to meet her during the day before the first day of school; the teachers hold open house for parents – and grandparents then," said the aide. "The music teacher hasn't been announced yet, so I don't have a name for you. Will Gerald be continuing our after-school soccer program?"

"Yes!" said GMR, as quick as a lighting bolt. "Do I get my old coach?"

"No, I'm sorry, that coach'll stay with the fourth graders. Gerald gets Miss Renfrew."

"A girl coach?" GMR was doubtful.

Lavinia settled her hand on his head. "Hush. Women are more famous for soccer in America than men."

The aide, gazing past them to the next parent, said, "Here's a list of the required school supplies and a schedule not only of the school-start-up but of all-the-school-holidays-and-dates-thank-you-very-much." She handed them paper and forced out a vacant smile.

"No, thank *you*. What do we say, GMR?"

"Thank you very much."

WHIT SWUNG ON BOARD THE bus and sussed out an empty seat close to the back, dropping the plastic grocery bag on the seat beside him. When the bus got to the Alvarado terminal he hopped off and slipped inside. Hiding in a stall in the restroom, he wiggled out of his auto-parts shirt, and slipped on a valet shirt, a jacket really.

He caught his transfer up San Mateo Boulevard, sitting up front behind the driver, and when his street rolled into view, he stepped forward. Rubbing the side of his nose Whit said, "I just missed my stop. Any chance you can drop me right here?" The driver glowered, but steered over to the curb. The doors slapped back, the bus dipped, and Whit got off.

A fast walk west on Osuna, a right on Brentwood and a saunter across the front and he was there – a gentleman's club on the north-east side of Albuquerque. High class booze and stripping. Whit ducked down behind the parking valet's stand in front. He spotted two real valets out in the lot under a tree, smoking and talking.

Whit opened the key cubby and checked for foreign car keys. As he found each one, he pressed the unlock button on the electronic fob and watched the lot to see each vehicle signal its location. He chose a German SUV parked close by and slid into it within thirty seconds. The valets were half-running toward him, one with his cell phone out.

At the edge of the lot, a new camera on a pole recorded his exit, as one had minutes before panned the front of the building and committed his image to digital storage – and a third had caught him at the SUV. He whipped south and west across town on the Interstates, as fast and as far as he could get. In a new industrial park full of beige metal buildings, the SUV wheeled up to "Bob's Auto Tint and Sound." Two sharp taps on the horn prompted the door to trundle up. Driving inside, he hopped out to find Two-Win's man alone in a bare garage.

"Petey, good to see you. Got another Kraut Coach for Tommy."

"Nice," said Petey as he inspected the vehicle. "Still smells new."

"Better get it into the truck soon. This one is way hot. It will be reported as stolen by now."

Petey frowned. "You handle your end, I'll handle mine."

Whit sniffled, rocked back a step. "Nothing intended. No need to get touchy." He scratched his nose. "You can give me a ride back to work, right? I need to go right now, I told 'em I'd be back by two."

CHAPTER TWENTY-FIVE

THE WEEKLY MEETING OF AABBA was in session in the sacristy of the Coventry Cross Baptist Church. The Reverend checked off his list. "Missus Chang, how are donations going?" He gave out his best smile, the one practiced for years to charm the parishioners.

Chang was the Asian of the neighborhood. A steely glare behind half moon reading glasses let anyone in her bakery know she wouldn't be jerked around. She could have been forty or eighty, without a trace of grey in her black, lustrous hair. "My son, he go roun' a' tha stores, put out coffee cans like this. Everybody like, but nobody have much money." She was holding out a can to the Reverend. It had a sheet of paper taped to it that said "Stop the Bridge," and on the other side it read "Association Against the Bosque Bridge of Albuquerque." A crude slot had been cut in the top of the golden plastic lid. "We raise forty two dolla'."

The Reverend gravely accepted a heavy paper bag full of one dollar bills and change. "I'm sure as things get closer, donations will pick up. Richard, what do you have to report?"

Richard had his giant forearms parked on the table, his chair pulled close to where his shirt buttons touched the table edge. "The bake sale tanked. An utter failure. The ladies tell me we were competing head-to-head with a Little League bake sale. Now I'm focused on a flea market to be held on Labor Day. We're short on the money we promised Harold—"

"I'll say," Harry threw in.

"As I mentioned," continued Richard with a frown, "we owe Harold for some radio time."

Raising his hand, Tenn said, "Tell us about the flea market."

"Well, for one thing, we've applied for a permit to block off the street in front of your place."

Tenn wrinkled his forehead so hard his eyebrows met. "You're asking the City to help you raise money to defeat the City?"

"Relax. The right hand won't know what the left is doing. We're already getting flea market donations. I'm storing them with people like Red Donnie and Jimmy's Garage. Some of it is 'surpassing strange.' Roger Kyber is giving all of his mother's clothes."

Harry said, "That's nice of him."

The pawnbroker shook his head, emphatic, rejecting. "It's disturbing. Who wears dead people's clothes?"

"The same people who pawn their mother's things with you."

Richard reared back in his chair.

"

, death
And lay me naked with no breath
Or borrow my shroud, stuck all with yew
Borrowed from no one so true.
Or something like that. Little Billy Shakespeare."

The Reverend cut in, "So, to summarize, we still need money, but in one week you have a fund raiser. How about you, Don?"

Red Donnie hung his head. "No luck. I've tried talking to any number of people. Most of them won't have anything to do with a protest rally. We're manning tables at the library and also at the grocery store, but it's hard to get people to stop and listen, much less sign a petition. The Sixties are dead." His ponytail swung around as he shook his head.

Halvard asked, "Is it just the wrong neighborhood?"

Donnie nodded. "I'll say. Some don't want to be anywhere near the police. Others have illegals in the family and don't want to attract any attention. Some are working two jobs and don't see how they would have the time. There are a few who are ready to chain themselves to the first bulldozer—"

"Really?" said the Reverend, his eyes opened wide.

"Metaphorically, of course. What we can do is hang up protest banners and posters, in shop windows, across storefronts. Bob Dobbel already has a home-made one up – he's still pissed off about the meeting with the Big Three."

Halvard tilted his head. "Well, that's a beginning. I'm sure you'll get some traction soon. How about you, Tenn? How is the legal battle going?"

Tenn replied, "No lawyer yet. We need one who will do it pro bono. In the meantime Soulful is acting as legal counsel. The City is moving ahead. The first right-of-way condemnation has happened, down and back of the River front."

Richard said, "They call it 'eminent domain.' Two beautiful words, abused."

Tenn nodded. "Means they give you some money and an eviction notice."

Halvard asked, "Is there any light at the end of the tunnel?"

Tenn replied, "The Catholics got their church on the historical list. That won't work for the rest of us though, except for a house here and there. My place was built in the fifties, like a lot around here."

The Reverend, sighing, said, "No, my church wouldn't qualify either."

Tenn said, "Soulful says we can slow things down with an injunction or two. It would buy us time. But we have to have a lawyer to file."

"I'll send out a call for legal help through the Southern Baptist Convention."

Tenn muttered to Richard, "I'd rather have an atheist as a lawyer."

Halvard ignored the whispering. "Now, Harry, the most important thing, public opinion. Come out shooting."

Harry shifted – uneasy on his round blue pillow. He grimaced a bit as he switched buttocks. "Good news and bad news. The liberals will be for us. We've been blogged under titles like 'A Bridge Too Far' and 'Save the Bosque Historic Neighborhoods.' We've got a tree-hugger at the paper on our side. Of course, he pisses off a lot of readers so he's a mixed blessing."

"And you said there was bad news?"

"Yes. Two pieces. The business journal is clearly for the bridge. Evidently the bridge will bring absolutely billions and billions of dollars into the economy. Meshugena pishers. And there's a new support group, the 'Bosque Bridge Boosters.' BBB. Some of our neighbors belong to that one."

Tenn asked, "What should we be doing now?"

Harry rolled his eyes. "More money for ads. More people wanting to cover the story. Radio and TV interviews. A great sound-bite from the Governor. A scandal in the Department of Transportation."

The Reverend replied, smiling and bobbing his head, "I'm sure you'll come up with something, Harry. We all have confidence in you."

THE OWNER OF CUT 'N Curl stopped Tenn on the sidewalk in front of Rip's. "Tenn, can we speak?"

"Mr. Russell. What can I do for you?"

"I've got a complaint, Tenn. It's your patrons."

"Oh?"

Mr. Russell nodded his shellacked head, waved a pair of scissors back and forth. "See here, the sidewalk has become a smoking zone. Lots of my customers have to come by your place, and look at it! A wasteland of cigarette butts. Your sidewalk and your planter, they're just nasty."

Tenn leaned away from the scissors. "Um, you've got a point."

"See, today is Monday and you're closed and it's still like this."

"You're right, Mr. Russell. I'll work harder at cleaning up."

"Good, that's all I wanted to hear." He dropped the scissors into the pocket of his sky-blue hairdresser coat. "How's the fight coming against City Hall?"

"Oh, so-so. We could sure do with your support."

"Still on the fence about this one, Tenn. That little shop up in northeast Albuquerque is looking better and better."

Tenn eked out a meager smile and turned away. Unlocking the front door, he proceeded into the gloom of his establishment. The boy's shoe lay in the middle of the floor, illuminated only by the beer sign over the bar. The other one might be anywhere – behind the bar, by the back door, upstairs.

CHAPTER TWENTY-SIX

HELEN PARCH'S CAR COOKED IN late afternoon. The windows' dark tint did little to block the heat falling like molten sky onto the car by the curb. Behind glass, behind sunglasses, the librarian afflicted with lust watched the boy on the sidewalk. Pale, hairy arms prickled with sweat. Drops of perspiration ran down her black hair, caught up in the collar, and collected in the elastic bands of her underwear. When GMR's lead stretched out to a block ahead, Helen turned on the vehicle. The air conditioning roared out a hot wind. The car crept forward for a block, slid in by the hydrant, and idled a second. She switched off and lingered in the heat, both hands rubbing into a cradle of seersucker pants, knuckles moving up her thighs. GMR stopped to talk to a dog, scruffed its ears, got the dog to sit. Such a nice child. What would it be like? So wrong. So good because it was wrong.

When GMR reached the strip, he stopped to squash his face up against the sheet glass of Cut 'N Curl, making a donut for his face with his hands. He waved at someone inside. Helen turned the key again and shifted into drive.

Whit Whittington rolled around the corner in his white beater of a car, turned directly towards the boy. GMR kept waving into the salon, trying to attract someone's attention. Whit saw the boy and jerked towards the curb. He popped his door open, stuck a leg out, and got set to chase.

Helen Parch saw the decrepit old car wrench over to the curb and a man spring out of the vehicle. It was the boy's father. No. He could not, would not have the child!

The moment hung there, quivering in the heat charged with possessive desires. With a rush, Helen gunned across the intersection like an arrow towards the white car. Front end and back end smashed, folded, and blew pieces of auto into the street. Neither car won. Her seat belt locked, her air bag deployed, while Whit squirted out onto the sidewalk, tumbling over and over to end scrunched up against stucco below a window.

GMR jerked around, shocked by the noise. His eyes flew open; his brain registered his father's car shoved up over the curb and his father sprawled on the sidewalk. He and his father stared at each other. GMR pivoted and ran up the block, past Rip's and on towards the Taquería. He sprinted in the front door and through the tables into the kitchen. Amos worked there, chef's knife in hand.

"Chico, what's up?"

"It's my Dad."

"Behind you?" The boy nodded. "Don't worry, he's not coming through here." Amos tapped the butt of the knife in his palm.

The boy asked, "Should I hide in here?"

"Cut back to Rip's through the alley and hide in your apartment. I come get you when it's safe, no?"

In the street outside, two people screamed at each other, both denied their opportunity.

IN THE MIDMORNING, THE FRONT door had been propped open. Three flies droned lazily overhead. A pawned fan hummed away, stirring tepid air around. Richard tried again. "It's called double-entry bookkeeping for a reason. See, there are two ledgers, so that's double. Each item or transaction gets entered twice, so that's double. The ledgers can be used to check each other for error, so that's double the protection. Double Entry Bookkeeping."

GMR asked, "So one ledger is?"

"Assets and Expenses." Richard wrote "assets and expenses" out on a yellow pad and drew a box around it.

"And the other ledger is?"

"Liabilities and Revenue." Richard wrote that out and boxed it.

"And everything has to happen twice?"

Richard said, "Right, you got it." He drew a circle and wrote "PT" inside. "Let's say I pay someone and give them a pawn ticket."

"Okay." The boy held up the pawn tablet, with its yellow and white pages.

"Then I write the amount I paid in the liability account as a negative number. I subtract it. I also write the amount as a plus number – I add it – in the asset account. "

GMR glanced at Richard, his eyes bugging out. "But you paid somebody money! How can paying be a plus?"

"Double also means backwards. When they pay me back, the money goes in as a negative number in Assets and a positive number in Liabilities." Richard beamed, held his hands out like a magician who had made a rabbit disappear.

"How do you know if you're making money?"

"Equity is assets minus liabilities."

"What's assets?"

"All this junk in here and the money in the drawer." Richard waved his hand about.

GMR screwed up his eyes. "I don't get it. Why don't you just count the stuff?"

This flummoxed Richard. "The secret is – always follow the rules."

GMR nodded, won over. "Rules are okay. If there's a rule, then you know."

"Follow the rules and the books balance." Richard held out both hands and waggled them up and down, then held them steady at the same level.

"Is that a good thing?"

"Oh yes."

"Will you write the rules down?"

"We'll tape them to the countertop glass right here. Someday soon you'll understand what we're doing."

GMR had a better answer. "I'll follow the rules. Then no one gets mad."

"And if I'm not mad, then I'll pay you."

"That's okay then."

"Double Entry is one of the mysteries of the universe." Richard leaned closer, confiding. "It was invented by a wizard named Luca Pacioli in the sixteen hundreds. I think it was the sixteen hundreds. He invented the system for the Medici Bank. He was a priest and a banker of course, like me. At least, the banking part." A fly lit on his forehead and the boy giggled. Richard swatted at his face with both hands.

"Maybe the fly doesn't know you're a banker."

CHAPTER TWENTY-SEVEN

IGNATIUS CALLOWAY MARCHED INTO RIP'S, bag slung across his shoulder. "Here's today's paper, Mr. Tenn. You're in it, on page four of section B." He opened the paper. "See, right here." He pointed with an ink-blackened finger. "It says, "Bar Fights Seemingly Hopeless Battle." That's you, right?"

Tenn sighed. "I suppose so. Another editorial declares us dead."

Calloway ran his hand up through the hair hanging in his face, letting it fall right back across his forehead. "My route manager pointed out the article. What battle is it? What's hopeless, anyway?"

"We don't want the bridge here, but they've already started spending highway money. The bridge is likely to happen."

"Oh. It's a big bridge, isn't it?"

"Bigger than Rip's. Want a limeade?"

"Can't. The *Journal* comes out 365 days a year, and I gotta make my rounds."

"I understand. How about I make you one to go, Cab? Surely you can spare a minute for that."

"Okay." He deposited his paper bag up on the bar, centered just so, and hopped up onto a barstool. "It's illegal for me to be in here? I should have a parent with me?"

"Something like that. Two or three years, though, you'll be able to sit there legally." Tenn snapped a plastic lid on the red plastic cup. "Here's your limeade."

"Is GMR here?"

"GMR, huh? No, he's in school right now. He won't be back for hours."

"I forgot. Well, I can come back later. When is he back?"

"About five, I think, after soccer. I didn't know you were friends."

"We play Dark Star Dungeon upstairs, in GMR's house." Calloway pointed at the ceiling. "I let him win, sometimes." He slipped off the stool and slung his bag over his shoulder. He snatched up the limeade. "I gotta make my rounds."

HELEN PARCH MAINTAINED A HIGH level of citizenship and part of citizenship included the local news. She didn't feel much like sorting through the political issues after her Friday stint at the Library, but she knew her responsibility, or at least her gravitas. Nobody had a better handle on facts than Madame Librarian. She snapped up the controller and got the PBS channel on, in time to get "Albuquerque in Review." This show centered on the struggle over the Bosque bridge. She sank gingerly down into her wingback chair – the whip-lash collar around her neck dug into the base of her ears.

The show's set was a simple table surrounded by a no-frills backdrop. Poorly lit gray curtains pretended to provide a black background and a sense of space. An earnest young man, barely out of journalism school, ran the discussion for the night and moderated a table of three people. Benjamin Taylor, Councilman for District Two, was ensconced to his right, grave and attentive. The Chinese woman named Chang who ran a bakery in the Bosque perched opposite him. To Helen's satisfaction, the third guest was Reverend Halvard. She caught the program at the moment where the Reverend said, "It's a way of life, and once it is gone, it will never come back."

Taylor said, "It's a low income neighborhood, not an endangered species. You're not all crested egrets down there."

"True," said the Reverend. "We weren't endangered until they surveyed out a bridgehead to run right through our living rooms. Now some of us feel our uniqueness and our way of life are under the gun."

"Come, don't exaggerate, Reverend. The bulk of the bridge footprint is in commercial space."

"But not a' of it," said the baker. "Many of us live where we work. Your office on very busy street, but your house in gated community miles away. Am I ri'?"

"As a matter of fact, I live in my district, on the edge of Nob Hill."

Her voice rose in pitch to high soprano. "Nob Hill. That Snob Hill, ri'? None of us live there. We on'y work there if we clean your house."

The moderator held both hands out, pushing back. "Now, Ms. Chang,"

"What my friend meant," the Reverend rushed in, "what I'm sure she meant, is that the Bridge will necessarily have a hard impact on people."

Taylor thrust four blue folders across the table at Halvard. "You say it will have a hard impact, but our studies show the bridge would be a tremendous economic boost, not only to Albuquerque but to the neighborhood itself."

Alone in her living room, Helen said, "There's always a stack of paper to prove anything."

On set, the Chinese baker shot back, "Not he'p us if we not live there anymore."

The camera shifted around to Taylor. He smiled the smile of reason. "The City and the County can guarantee a fair price for any property they have to acquire. We want to be fair, but we also want to be thinking about what is best for Albuquerque."

"Fair price to landlords," said Chang. "What about renters, li' us?"

Across the set in the control booth, the director said into his mike, "God, I hate this show. The Shopping Channel is more exciting." He tapped his fingers and considered. "Time for some fun. Jerry, I'm cutting to your camera, cam 2. Brighten it until the Rev shines."

A shift in the camera angle revealed the back of the Reverend's head, exposing his bald spot with its comb-over. The camera also caught the Chinese woman in profile, emphasizing her epicanthic eyes, her yellow face with flaring nostrils stretched out like a horse. The Reverend's shiny spot flared into the camera as he nodded and made his point. "We understand your position and it sounds reasonable. However, the *people* don't wish to have this bridge."

Taylor waded in. "Not all the people are against the bridge, Reverend. I think the Boosters for the Bosque Bridge would support me in that, if they had been invited." He shot a glance at the moderator.

The moderator said, "We contacted BBB, but they couldn't send any one in time. Their president sends his regrets that he can't make it down from Rio Rancho this evening.

"Ha." Chang jumped on the mention of Rio Rancho. "They don't live where we live. They live a' over town."

"And this is an Albuquerque bridge, not just your bridge," answered Taylor. The camera showed him tanned and healthy in appearance, his blue shirt collar starched.

Halvard tried again, "There must be an amicable way to avoid uprooting these people." His coat collar had a flap folded under and his shirt rumpled up against the back of his neck.

"Exactly why we have been conducting our community meetings."

"You come, but you not listen." Chang trembled. Whether the shakes were from nervousness or anger, the camera didn't care.

Halvard plodded on. "If we would move the bridge south to the Botanical Gardens, the bridge would only impact a neighborhood on one side of the River, not two."

"It's the Botanic Garden, by the way." Taylor gave a wry smile for the camera.

Halvard had been caught off guard. "What?"

In her living room, Helen said, "It's the Botanic, you fool."

Taylor pressed home. "The Botanic, not the Botanical. It's also called the Biopark. The Botanic represents fifteen years of sustained effort and committed development on behalf of our children and our families."

Halvard tried to catch up. "Fifteen years while the rest of the river front was sadly neglected." The camera remained directed at the Reverend's bald spot and on past, to the Councilman's face.

"Oh, come now. Your neighborhood probably uses more City resources than most. Emergency care, social services, police protection, crisis counseling. Food stamps."

"You care more about the zoo tha' you care about us," said the baker. Halvard shot her a warning glance.

"I think my record speaks for itself. I have always served with the best interest of Albuquerque and her people in mind."

Helen in her living room hissed at the TV.

The moderator broke in, "Before we have to close, I want to ask each of you, what in your mind is the best outcome for this issue. What common ground do you see? Ms. Chang, if you would go first." He beamed as if something good had just happened, nodded to the woman.

"My best outcome is my bakery left a' alone. I keep serve my customers."

"Reverend?"

"In truth? The City redirects the bridge elsewhere and then treats this neighborhood as an equal to other places in Albuquerque."

"Councilman?"

"Best result? That this Bosque neighborhood profits from the jobs and the development that comes with the bridge, thanks to governmental entities who have brought it a magnificent gift. Oh, and I wouldn't mind being re-elected in three years." He grinned for the camera, letting it in on the joke.

People on and off set laughed, but not Chang and Halvard. And not Helen.

ROGER KYBER THOUGHT THE STREET showed its wear and tear even more than usual – of course early morning had that effect. The grit under his feet sounded like the grit in the corners of his eyes felt. A newspaper blew around in the alcove of Enchanted Valley Cash 4 U. He picked the page up and stuffed it absently into the pocket of his big coat. The cold had bitten into him on his front step, but now after the hike over to Julio's, he sweated. And the leg hurt worse.

Julio's Taquería could have hunkered down on a street in Ensenada or Nuevo Laredo. The front was sheathed all in glass, except where the takeout window formed a half-wall and countertop. Julio had covered the bottom of the glass in photos of food mounded on plates; the sun had not been kind to the colors. The top two feet of glass were dedicated to menus. This left a two-foot, chest-high view into the establishment. Like everyone in the neighborhood, Roger never read the menus – he knew everything they made, including the specials never listed. Above the window, an awning cast its beneficent relief onto the store front. Above that hung Julio's pride and joy, the neon sign.

Roger slid in the door, let it draw shut behind, and hit him on his heels and butt. He scanned the room, an old military habit. Ambling across the floor first to the coffee machine behind the counter, he pulled a mug. Backing it up with a paper cup full of water, he parked the two on his favorite table. He ignored three people who also sat there. He returned behind the counter to find a large flour tortilla. He smeared it with frijoles, carne adobada, and queso fresco. Three more steps and he arrived at an industrial strength microwave; he melted the cheese. Taking a sheet of wax paper out of a box, he retrieved the burro and trudged to his table.

Once seated, he glared at the three young people until they slid away, taking their coffee with them.

Julio appeared to clear the remnants of their meal. "Buenos días, Roger. Scaring away my customers?" He stacked the three plates up in one hand and mopped the table with a wet towel.

"Morning, Julio. You're the scary one. I'm not ex-gang."

Julio's predatory teeth flashed. He resembled some thin, tight-wound beast about to make a kill. He was field-worker dark and a burn scar ran pink up one arm. The bottom half of his left ear had disappeared years ago. "Me, I'm mi madre's hijo. All leche y galletas."

Roger fished in his front pocket. "Here's the five."

"You gone to this much trouble, maybe you should drop it in the register, ring it up."

"Maybe I should tip myself too."

Julio rocked back on his heels, craned his head down and sideways like a turtle. "You look like shit, soldado."

"Up most of the night."

Julio eased down across from Roger. "Yeah, we can tell."

"I was boxing up my Mother's stuff. Real slow going."

"Qué?"

"She kept everything. She had a photo of me at the enlistment office."

"Which of your wars, Korea or 'Nam?"

"Korea. Funny thing. She was the one found out about me and my buddies and our vandalism. She was the one drug me down to the recruiters by the ear. And she was the one who was proud when we both signed the forms."

"Chu underage back then?"

"Just a year. If she had known anything about the real Army, she wouldn't have forced me into it. Anyway, slow going. I found my letters from Viet Nam about one a.m., just sat there reading them again, all the way through to the ones from the hospital."

"Best to let that type of thing go, hermano."

Roger made a 'cha' sound. "Like you and Amos are letting go?"

"Your eyes all red, Roger. I think you been crying some."

"Naah, the pollen count is back up this morning. I got the crying done when we buried her. Thanks, by the way, for coming out. I didn't talk to you at the graveside."

"De nada. I liked your mom."

"She liked you too."

"Tough woman, puttin' up with you all these years."

"Not so much. She was a saint."

Julio snorted and then shaped his face into an apology. "Sorry. I chust thought about the time she was wailing on old Mrs. Sandoval. We hear it two blocks over. Policía din' like that one."

Roger grinned. "Things got tough for her after my father died. But my mother was a saint."

"Here, let me get some coffee." Julio left for a moment, got coffee, and waited on a customer who wanted a burrito to go. "So, I figured out your fix-it shop is not open these days. I got a dishwasher seize up and begin leaking. Thought I would bring it by. But your door is closed and the blinds is drawn."

"Yeah, I haven't felt much like opening these days."

"Is it the Bridge?" Julio said this offhanded, staring out the front window.

Roger rubbed his eyes. "I don't know. First Ma and then the neighborhood."

"Sí. Be good to find a way to stand up and be counted."

"And get knocked down."

—⁓—

THE DEVIL WAS DRIVING HER crazy. When Ilene McKennet was crazy she cooked. The kitchen had heated up to a hundred, with the oven coils glowing through the glass door. The air conditioning in the front room wheezed and spit, but none of its solace reached into this room. She worked at the kitchen table, white hams of her forearms on the edge of the cutting board in front of her, holding a carrot and peeling it while she thought about the Devil and about Cheezsy. Perspiration added funk to the vanilla smell of cake that was baking. Ilene didn't call him Cheezsy – she preferred his real name. Not like proper names could help. No doubt about it, Milo was doomed to Hell. Not only did he deny Jesus Christ the Lord, but he was one of those who had crucified the Savior.

The Devil sprawled across the tabletop, his cheek resting on his hand, his knee up in the air. He poked at her elbow with a long, sharp fingernail. "Doomed. Nothing you can do about it. He and his people are all mine." He wore a suit today and had encased his hooves in fine, polished leather – wing-tip shoes, cordovan colored.

She replied, "A good Christian woman can turn around a bad man."

"And you call yourself a Christian woman? You sure have a broken view of *that* concept." His breath feathered out, stinking sharp like turpentine.

"I am a Christian!"

"Like you pay attention to that? Eager to see him, eager to wallow in a bed of sin." The Devil smacked his lips, "Sin. I do love it so. I eat it up, just like I'll eat you up."

She jerked her head up towards him. "I'm not really a sinner. I'm only trying to save a good man."

"By folding him in your arms? Nestling his little body down between your legs?" The Devil slid his index finger back and forth in a ring made with his other hand's thumb and forefinger.

She jerked her eyes away from his ugly gesture. "Love-making gets him to listen."

The Devil, brown and wrinkled, snickered at her. "Don't fool yourself. You love it. You're the merry widow, right enough." He drummed his heel on the table, snickered some more.

"I find great joy with Milo Brezinski, sex or no sex."

"Carnal joy with Cheezsy Brezinski. And you're delusional. You hope to become Mrs. Milosovich Brezinski one day."

"Maybe." She hung her head.

"Cheezsy given you any encouragement that way?"

"No. Not a word."

The Devil held his hand up, index finger pointed at the ceiling. "So, don't lie. Tell me the truth. Tell *Gawd Almighty* the truth." He wagged that finger.

"I do it with him because I want to. I do IT." A single tear ran down her face, dripped onto her bosom.

"And the truth will set you free! Hallelujah!"

"Go away. Don't do this today."

"Any day is a good day for sin. You're waiting now for him to call, aren't you? Unredeemed, unredeemable."

She murmured, "My Lord, who art in heaven."

"Prayer doesn't help when it's empty. You have to redeem yourself, or you'll end up in my hands." He reached out his claw and traced a line on her cheek with his dirty fingernail. "I'll drink up all your tears."

Chapter Twenty-Eight

RICHARD WAS INSTALLED AT THE bar like a municipal sculpture, this time with a Black Russian planted in front of him. Beside him perched GMR, with an orange juice on ice in a lowball. GMR had a swizzle stick. Richard had a hangover.

Richard asked, "What's your name again?"

"Gerald Matthew Roger Whittington."

"Might want to change that Whittington. You don't have much to do with that part of your name now."

The boy remained silent.

"My full name is Richard Mattias Martin. Mattias means Matthew."

The boy's face broke out in a smile. "We have the same name."

"I got the Matthew part from a saint, I expect. People name their children for saints hoping they'll grow up to be a little bit better than the last generation."

"What's a generation?"

"All the people born in the same ten years or so. A generation's a group of everybody clear across the world, except it's a fake group. Those people don't have anything in common besides birth years."

"Is it like a grade in school?"

"More or less."

They both sipped their drinks. Richard said, "Lavinia says you're in trouble at school right now."

"Yes."

"What's that about?"

"I've been late. Four times. I have trouble getting up."

"It gets worse, not better, as you get older," replied Richard.

The boy gave him an alarmed glance. "Really?"

"Maybe. Maybe not. So what happens at school?"

"They have a rule. If you don't follow it, then you have to go to the Principal's office. You miss the first part of class. And they give you a note to take home to your parents."

"That's a bit awkward."

"Yes. Mr. Tenn signs it."

"Why do you call him Mr. Tenn?"

"Because he told me to."

Richard swirled the Black Russian. "So, do you want an alarm clock for your apartment?"

"Miss Lavinia gave me one. I forget to turn it on sometimes."

"School is some distance away, isn't it?"

"Yes."

"So you wake up late, you run most of the way to school, and you still get sent to the Principal's office."

The boy nodded.

"Tough break." They both picked up their drinks, stared down into the ice. "Want some help on this?"

"What kind of help?"

"How about I drive you to school every day? I could come over fifteen minutes early, make sure you're up."

GMR's face split into a grin. "That would be really good."

"Do you like frozen waffles?"

RICHARD'S ALARM BEEPED IN A calypso rhythm, but he continued to lie comatose, a massive lump. A second alarm jangled within the minute, a loud ugly alarm. He heaved himself up, fought both alarms, and sighed as deep as the Grand Canyon. "Beelzebub's machines, I swear. And I'm talking to myself again."

In the bathroom, he leaned in to stare at himself in the mirror, belching and thrusting out his tongue. "Strange. I expected to see actual fur."

He carried his toothbrush and his razor with him into the shower and scratched at his stubble while the hot water ran down his broad back. "Christ, I haven't been up at six since I was in school." He brushed his teeth and spat the toothpaste into the tub around his feet.

Once dressed, Richard shuffled to his refrigerator, delved in the freezer for a box of waffles, and nestled them into a plastic bag. A toaster from his pawnshop inventory already hid in there. The bag slumped on the counter right beside the bottle of vodka. His large swollen finger prodded the bottle.

He normally had the first one at eight. Only six forty-five. "It's okay. I can wait. I don't mind. The hell I don't mind!" He banged the vodka back against the splash-block, snorted, and picked up the toaster bag.

As he dropped into his old tank of a car, Richard fished in his pants for the keys. His gaze swept around at the stark sideways light of early morning and he proclaimed,

"Like the skylark,
our sweetest songs tell of our sleepiest thoughts.
We ascend to greet the new day
ober and resolute."

RICHARD PARKED IN THE ALLEY behind Rip's, blocking it with his huge sedan. Huffing up the stairs, he leaned over with his hands on his knees and panted a bit at the top before knocking on the door.

GMR opened the door a crack, peeked around the edge to see, and swung it back in welcome. The boy wore jeans and a T-shirt, and his book bag lay in the hall.

Richard said, "Your hair's a mess. Go comb it and I'll start breakfast. The boy trotted down the hall into the bathroom and Richard proceeded into the kitchen. He plugged in the toaster, populated it with his waffles, and set two paper towels out on the chipped table. The fridge revealed jelly but not margarine. Banging the jar down on the table, he swiveled away to find a silverware drawer and a knife, picking at the blade with a finger nail, scratching at the blemish where the plating had come off. Rust had arrived. Real life.

They ate without words, crunching through the waffles and wiping their mouths with the paper towels. Richard shoved back his chair; it made a discordant screech on the linoleum. "Time to go. We don't want to be late, especially after all I've been through."

As Richard descended the stairs, the boy locked his door, and springing down the steps, bounced into the car. GMR clicked his seatbelt and gripped his book bag in his lap. "You should fasten your seatbelt. There's a law and you could get in trouble."

With a heavy sigh Richard felt around for his belt, and grunting, jerked it across himself. "And Lo the child shall instruct the man, and so shall the man earn the Gates of Heaven."

"You talk real funny."

"And you speak ungrammatically. What time do I pick you up?"

"After soccer?"

"Christ."

"I can walk back."

"No, if I'm going to do this, I'll do this. Show me where the soccer field is and tell me what time." As they eased onto the street, Richard said, "There's your Mom's car. Duck down in the seat."

—*—

ON THE KITCHEN TABLE AMIDST the crumbs, afternoon drinks crowded up between them. A beer and a tequila, a Mexican brandy, and a small dopp kit, zipped shut, rested close by their elbows. Whit inched the tequila shooter around from the left hand to the right and back. He had a square bandaid taped to his temple and his elbows showed off similar patches. Intienda asked, "Are you sure?"

"Oh, yeah. They showed up at work. Harv called me right after the squad car left."

"Are they sure it's you?"

"They showed a photo of me in front of the club, and they had my booking shot from five years ago."

She picked up the brandy and swigged down a large swallow. "How can they link it together so quick?"

"Computers, I guess." His voice shook. "I don't like the idea of more jail time."

Intienda picked up on the shake, and reached across the table to cuddle his hand. "So, what are we going to do?"

"I think it's time for us to move. They'll be here soon: maybe they're already on the way."

"No, they won't show up here. The lease is in my maiden name."

"You think they don't know we're married?" Whit and Intienda leaned their heads together. "Damn, I feel boxed in."

Her face relaxed and her thin lips hooked up in a smile – she had a way out of the box. "Two-Win? Maybe Tommy can move us out to L.A. and get us started again."

"I called. The little gook cut me loose."

"Ahhh. He seemed so sweet," she said with a soft voice.

He threw the shooter back and slurped on his beer. "Can't use my car – besides, the wreck pretty much destroyed the back end. I'll steal an old clunker, drive over to Arkansas. Talk to a cousin. When the police get here, tell them I've been gone for a few days. Tell 'em I often come and go without letting you know much."

"What about us? Me and the kids?"

"Just sit tight. I'll get us a house, find some job, and figure out who runs the local chop shop. Then I'll call and you can disappear."

"We're out of real money, Whit."

He opened his wallet, doled out three hundred dollars. "Last of the car insurance settlement. Cheese and macaroni time, baby. We done it before." He shoved back from the table. "I better hurry and pack. One other thing, baby. Find GMR. I can't leave my boy behind."

CHAPTER TWENTY-NINE

INTIENDA HADN'T BEEN HERE BEFORE. Whit had always provided money from the auto store or another car theft so it had never been necessary. She froze in front of Enchanted Valley Cash. How did pawning something work? There had to be a pattern, but she didn't have a clue what to do or what to say.

She almost turned away, gave up. The thought of her little girl held her there, pinned to the sidewalk. She imagined taking Amy in through the front door of the school, the special school. Intienda imagined her daughter cooing, squeezing her hand, laughing at the bright walls and colorful murals, and pictured a woman sweeping up and leaning down to beam into the face of her child, kneel and talk to her.

When she opened the door, she had trouble dragging the luggage into the shop. The huge man behind the counter brought his head up when the bell on the door rang and stared with interest at a new person. "Can I help you?"

She could hear her breath rattling in her throat, could hear her heartbeat. "Yes, I brought in a few things to pawn."

"We prefer to call it a collateralized loan."

She shot him a glance – those words meant nothing.

"Well, then, what do you have?"

She struggled to place the roll-on up on the counter. "It's real Gucci. And I have the full size down here."

"So I see. Very elite luggage." He checked quick, subtle to make sure they weren't Chinese knock-off.

"Thank you. I've got some other things." From the roll-on, Intienda brought out two cut glass brandy decanters and a pair of hand-tooled boots.

Richard cleared his throat, stared up into the corner.

"I'll pawn

My hopes of Heaven - you know what they are worth,

That the presumptuous landlords of Earth,

Would give up Paradise's dove -

Folly can season Wisdom, and Hatred Love."

Her forehead wrinkled like a prune. She shook her head, as if the verse had been a fly that lit and then buzzed off. She glanced up from the roll-on, held up a decanter for his inspection.

Richard reached out a hand to accept the cut glass. "Keats. Or maybe Byron."

"Please, how much? I'm trying to put together an enrollment fee. Two thousand. For my daughter. For a special school."

Richard wheezed a bit. It was a mistake, but she did look pathetic. "The boots are quite nice. I don't normally handle clothes, but I'll say one fifty for them. Five each for the cut glass. Two hundred for the bags."

"Two hundred each?"

"No, I'm sorry, dear. Two hundred all together."

"But the bags alone cost a thousand." Or would have, if they hadn't come off the back of a truck. "And the boots are Rio Tesoro!"

"No doubt, dear thing. I can give you cash now, or you can try to sell them elsewhere. Perhaps online."

She needed money now. Two thousand. A tear spilled out of her eye.

Richard jerked back, appalled by her emotion. "All right, all right. I'll throw in another fifty. But it costs you ten percent when you redeem them."

"Oh. Casi una quarta parte. Okay." She held on to the counter edge soundless and bent while he filled out the pawn details and handed her the tickets. Taking them gingerly, she held them close to her eyes and read them through. What the remaining one thousand six hundred meant, she knew. It meant prostitución again. Hooking.

Richard heaved himself off the stool and stumped to the register. He brought the money back and counted out four hundred and ten dollars into her hand.

Now audibly sobbing, she thrust it in her bag and hurried out of the shop. The door slapped shut.

"Damn! Misery acquaints a man with strange women." Back on his stool, Richard made no move to shelve Intienda's things. Feeling a pressure deep in his chest, burning a bit, centered on his esophagus. He murmured to the pain, "Ah, my old nemesis Angina, starving my best friend of Oxygen." He fumbled in his front pocket, reaching in under the bulge of fat that hid the top of his pants. "Nitroglycerin, most explosive of all treatments, friend to the dilatory." Pouring a pill out of the prescription bottle and placing it under his tongue, he felt better in a moment, when the pain eased off.

"Well, that's that," he said into the room. "Ave Caesar, morituri te salutant. Only I'm not going to die, not just yet. Well, Caesar, we should still toast you. He held the chipped wine glass out at chest level and gazed into its clear contents. The glass ascended to his lips, as if unbidden.

THEY COULD SMELL ONE OF the horse ranches on the River burning leaves. Acrid, reassuring, home-like. Amos thought it smelled like the Afghan poppy fields after harvest, when the morphine farmers burnt them off.

"See," said Red Donnie. "This is easy. They don't dare run over us." He wrapped the chain around Rhonda's ankle and locked it. Then he locked her to a steel ring on the bulldozer's blade. Amos and Calloway imitated him. All four dropped down onto the curb. Behind them the cottonwoods choked the edge of the River. The sun cut across them sharp and bright; the faint chilly breeze toyed with them. It promised to be a clear, crisp fall day.

"Now what?" asked Amos. His head swiveled right and left as he scanned up and down the street. He humped his shoulders up, to be smaller and less exposed. Too out in the open.

Red Donnie said, "We wait. The crew won't start work until eight, and the newspaper and TV people will also show up about then."

"This is against the law isn't it?" Rhonda didn't have the guise or guile of a criminal.

"Maybe yes, maybe no," Red Donnie answered.

Calloway said, "Wait – you said demonstration. You didn't say anything about breaking the law." He jumped up and scurried away from the bulldozer as far as the chain would let him. "I could lose my job!"

"Naah, the dozer is on public right of way. We're not trespassing," said Amos. His head still ticked, left, right, left.

Red Donnie said, "Might as well sit down, Iggy. I brought coffee." A brown bag on the curb – he dug into it. "God, I love this. It's just like the old days. Lying down in front of the troop trains.

189

Chaining ourselves to the doors of the Admin building."

Rhonda glanced at her wristwatch. "Seven thirty. A half hour until eight. I wish I had gone to the bathroom first."

They never got to the coffee. Two pickups rolled up, doors with logos popped open and four men in safety vests jumped out, real, immediate. It was about to happen. "Yo. Whatcha doing there?"

"We're from the neighborhood," said Red Donnie. His voice rang high, bright. "This is a protest. You can't come through here. You can't bulldoze our homes and businesses."

The oldest guy, a toffee-colored black, said, "My name is McDonnel. I'm the crew chief here. I need to ask you to move on."

"Can't," replied Amos. He held up his leg and shook the chain. "We're here to stay." He liked the thrashing, ringing sound, so he shook the chain again.

McDonnel turned to one of his guys and said, "Call 911." While the minion did his bidding, he swiveled back to Amos. "Okay, gimme the keys."

Red Donnie got the ring out of his pocket, jangled the padlock keys together, and hurled them towards the River into the trees. "Too late."

"Wise ass. Okay, we wait." The road gang stepped back to their vehicles, clustered up in a circle, and watched the foursome. They made more phone calls. Twenty-five minutes for the squad car to arrive. One officer consulted with the workers and one visited with Donnie. More talking. Going round again, the police spoke to each other, then to McDonnel, then again to Red Donnie.

Red Donnie said to his cop, a mere youngster, "Go ahead, push us around. The People will be heard."

The cop shook his head. "What do you think this is, Pop? Here's what'll happen. These guys will cut you loose from the dozer *at the dozer*, nowhere near you – no muss no fuss. You can do what you want with the chains once these guys got their property back. I'd ask you to move along and not block any legal activities here."

McDonnel and one of his men approached with bolt cutters from a pickup tool chest and sheared the chains at the blade. "Fire her up," he instructed his man. Planting himself in front of Red Donnie, he continued, "I see the press is here. But now you look a little pitiful, don't cha? Skinny mo-fo shit."

As the camera truck spilled out a cameraman and reporter, Donnie mobilized his team. "Stand in front here. Link arms." They did so, Amos checking out how the other three would react. He could tell Calloway was as swept up in the moment as Rhonda, and Red Donnie was ecstatic. They faced the crew, resolute, the dozer blade at their back. The dozer did indeed start, with the farting sounds of a diesel at low rpm. A stink of half-burnt fuel filled the air.

One of the officers stepped up to Amos' shoulder and lightly punched him on the arm. "Come on, buddy. It's over. Step away and nothing has to happen."

Screwing up his eyes, Amos said, "Don't touch me."

"What? What did you say?"

Throwing out his chest and sucking up his big belly, Amos repeated, "Don't touch me." His voice rose in volume and pitch.

"Okay, that's it, buddy. Assume the position." The cop manhandled Amos towards the dozer blade as he got out his handcuffs.

Amos shrugged off Rhonda's arm. "I said, don't you goddamn touch me! Chingado, nobody never touches me!" Amos pivoted on his feet towards the cop. The man stepped back, clawing at his belt for his nightstick. Amos drove his fist deep into the officer's belly and as the man folded, rammed his thick forehead into a soft, vulnerable, official nose.

The cameraman caught it all on video for the afternoon news.

The final closing shot showed Amos on his face in the dirt with the second officer cuffing him, while Amos' friends milled around. Rhonda bleated, Calloway bemoaned his job, and Donnie reassured Amos, "It's okay man. They seized our Lord just like you and it was righteous. They beat you man, that was awesome! The Lord will give you comfort and He'll help us bail you out."

ACROSS THE DESK FROM BEN Taylor, Reverend Halvard slumped deep in the chair, as passive as his rumpled clothes. "Thanks for meeting with me, Councilman."

Taylor said, "Well, it's not like I don't feel sorry for you. Your little group is pretty much finished, isn't it?"

"Oh, we'll get past this."

"Come on, Reverend. What small amount of leverage you had disappeared when your man beat up an Albuquerque policeman."

"My man is a veteran. He has PTSD. He got it in Afghanistan, serving his country."

"Not what the VA says."

"He over-reacted. He felt threatened."

"The cop is the one who should have felt threatened." The Councilman stretched expansively. "Like I said, you're done. I get my bridge, *and* I get to make a little speech about Respect for Our Men in Blue on the five o'clock news. You get squat."

Halvard held out his palms. "You represent us too. We're your constituents also."

"Yes, that's true. And I bet none of your low-class neighborhood voted for a conservative like me. It's a good thing you're such an impotent pussy." Taylor smirked.

A red flush shot up into the Reverend's face. "We've wanted to make this work for everybody, from the very first. I just want to keep my church."

Taylor leaned back in his chair, folded his hands over his protruding stomach. "And we gave you all due consideration. All you had to do was bend over and grab your ankles."

Halvard's voice rose in anger. "You gave us nothing. Not one thing! You practically pistol-whipped us!"

"Sorry you see it that way. Us elected officials have to make hard decisions sometimes. People want leaders. Not noisy little pukes like you."

"Hard decisions? It wasn't hard for you at all. You walk all over me and you shit on me. But you don't know who I am. No one knows who I am."

"Oh, come now. Everybody knows who you are. You're the loser here, and now you're playing the victim. Look at yourself – pretty pathetic."

"You can't talk to me that way!"

"A little cry-baby. Waaa."

Halvard leapt to his feet. "No, I think you're going to be the baby." He reached behind his back and brought out a shining revolver from the small of his back. It looked monstrous in his hand. "See! Now I'm in charge!"

"Jesus, man! What are you doing?" Taylor thrust himself back violently from the desk, his chair banging into the wall behind him.

"I'm finishing this, that's what!" One bullet tore past Taylor's head. As Halvard fired on the recoil, one streaked into the ceiling. The next shot died in the desk and the fourth destroyed the phone. Only with the fifth bullet, but not the wild sixth, did Halvard manage to plug Taylor in the gut.

CHAPTER THIRTY

TENN FOUND THE ALCOHOL SMELL in Rip's particularly unsettling. Even after booze is run through the still, it has that metallic tang of yeast buried somewhere back inside the smoky, seductive smell. The *Albuquerque Journal* lay on the bar, open to the front page and the Reverend. All Halvard's story now, and not the bridge. AABBA and its cause were forgotten, and even the ultra-liberals were now wrapped up in the shooting story on "EyeWitness News." They all wanted to hear more titillating detail about this Man of God who packed a revolver.

Tenn poured out a shot of bourbon and eased it down by the *Journal* like setting it on an altar. Spreading both hands out on the paper, he stared deep into the photo of Halvard – Halvard hanging his head in shame as he was escorted from the building, humped up, hands cuffed behind him. Tenn stared hard enough to change the photo, willing it to transform into a picture of something else. Perversely, it refused and hung on to the same discouraging image. Sighing, he straightened up and touched the shot glass with his fingertips.

Restless, he wandered to the front door. Outside a huge yellow front-end loader trundled by, tires dwarfing the parking meters in front of Rip's. It belched out diesel fumes in a black plume and turned left for the River. And the bridge site. His hand struck the glass of the door, a thud of anger, and his head shook like it was throwing off a punch. It was done.

The chime on the dishwasher brayed out. He emptied it, dried a few residual spots, returned glasses to their racks, then paced down the bar past the *Journal*, and the shot. His hand grazed along the edge of the counter. He jerked a bag of ice out of the freezer by the back door. All the way to the ice tub, his eyes stayed fixed on the glass. Tenn poured the ice into the prep sink and chopped at it with short savage blows from the ice pick.

REGINA SAID, "JUANITA IS GONE." She wished they had met at the Taquería instead of Rip's. Her hunger gnawed at her so bad, she had the shakes. At least her wrists and forearms looked better. Boney.

Harry picked at the rough finish on the table with a thumbnail. "Who the hell is Juanita?"

"GMR's big sister. I've seen her fighting with her mother."

"So? So she's gone."

"So I've been spying on them. When I didn't see her for a week, I made it my business."

Susan McNally cocked an eyebrow. "Regina, what did you do?"

"I snuck over to their house and snooped around. No cars, the back door unlocked, and nobody home. What a dump."

"What did you find out?"

"I found Juanita's phone number on a bill and I texted her."

"And?"

"This is really serious. She said that bad men had her locked up. She said that they had threatened to kill her father. She said her mother had sold her to the men."

Harry snorted, waved a dismissive hand. "That's just bullshit."

"Maybe. That's why I'm only talking to you and Susan about it. Here, let me show you the messages – I didn't delete them."

"Huh." He scrolled down. "Okay, she typed it, but that doesn't mean she's not lying." Harry frowned, continued to scroll up and down in the messages.

Susan said, "It happens more'n you think, Harry. Women and particularly underage girls, girls of color, get sold into prostitution."

"This part of your GLBT defense league?"

Regina stepped up. "Harry, there are billboards up on I-25 about this. It's part of Albuquerque's dirty underbelly."

"So why didn't she call 911?"

Regina slapped the table. "Be dead or gone before the police got in to her, wouldn't she?" She was certain.

He shifted uneasily, tried for a comfortable seat. "So why does this Juanita still have the phone?"

"Next message on the thread. She hid the phone. Juanita used the map app to find where she is and tell me." Regina paused. "What if it's real?"

Susan said, "The police ain't never gonna take this seriously."

Harry confirmed, "No judge is going to issue a warrant based on this fantasy."

"Let's go and see, see if she's lying. Or telling the truth," said Susan.

"Us?" Regina asked. "Two women and a scrawny old Jew?"

Harry frowned at the "scrawny" part. He slapped a glance towards Regina, swung his head to Susan. "Not our job."

"GMR ain't our job either. And I notice you bought him school supplies."

"Not our job," repeated Harry. "But I know who might take it on."

———

THE TWO WOMEN AND HARRY huddled at the back table in Julio's Taquería with Amos Armenez. Julio had painted the walls that peculiar southwest turquoise. The color combined with the cool fluorescent lights to make the two whites at the table appear pasty green. Amos wore a dirty chef's apron over a white T-shirt. A big bandage hung over his left eyebrow where the nightstick had split him open. He handed the phone back to Regina. "So, why you showing me this?"

"We thought you might have some ideas," said Regina.

"Qué pues?" he asked.

"You know. About how to find out."

"You want somebody to go see. Figure out if this girl is being muled out as a puta."

Susan shook her head. "No. We want someone to go who could get her out."

"And you chose a fat old cook because?"

Harry said, "I told them you like guns." Amos raised his eyebrows. "And that you knew how to kick in doors and search houses."

Amos held his hands out, in a gesture that said, So?

"And I told them the war had made you a little crazy."

Amos replied, "That's not for you to say." He didn't raise his eyes to the three people, but stared, eyes fixed on the honey dispenser on the table. "You got nerve, asking me to do this. Mierda, I'm out on bail now."

Regina said, "The girl is Latina."

Amos smiled – just a twitch in the corner of his mouth. "You must care a lot, to make a cheap try like that."

197

"You don't think you could do it?" Regina asked.

"What, take the law into my own hands?"

"Yes, that's pretty much it."

"Of course I *could* do it. I have a friend who served in Afghanistan – he'd do anything for me. And I'd bring Roger Kyber, Tenn's friend. He got messed around in Korea and messed up in 'Nam. We all got guns."

Harry asked, "What about your brother Julio?"

"He was a medic, man. He never shot no one."

"Oh. I thought with the gang stuff and the military."

"Naah. Not Julio. He's a softie. He just looks bad-ass."

Amos got up and scuffed over to the takeout window, leaned on the counter. They didn't know what he saw out on the street, but when he shambled back, he said, "We could do it."

"Will you?" asked Susan. "It has to happen quick."

Amos shot a glance around the table, stared up at the florescent. He shuffled his feet, turned in his chair. "This is criminal conspiracy, isn't it?"

Harry answered, uneasy. "Yes."

"And if I get her back you don't know what happens next, do you?"

"No." Regina sighed, glanced down at the table top.

Amos scratched his chin. His lips twisted. "Chure, I'll take it on."

All three dropped their mouths, opened their eyes wide. Regina asked him, "Why?"

"The war. It's right here every day, calling me."

———

THEY MET IN PLAIN SIGHT, three men and two cars, in front of the Taquería at midnight. Amos spread the map out on the hood of the car, shown a flashlight on it. "It's here. 12804. Roger been watching the place all afternoon and evening.

Roger tapped his finger on the map. "An old closed-down music store. Regular businesses on each side – they're shuttered up now for the night. Two, maybe three men, a couple of vehicles. Something definitely wrong there, but I didn't see the little girl."

"Ah knew it was a music store from my phone." Susan marched up and held her smart phone out to them. Google Street View shown out in the dark.

"Susan," said Amos. "You shouldn't be here."

"I'm goin' along. She's comin' with me afterwards."

Amos replied, "Huh. Well. Okay, you follow us in, but only when I say. You take care of la chica, nothing else."

"What's your plan?" she asked.

"We'll try walking in. If the door is locked, we'll kick it in."

"That's it?"

"No es rocket science." He waved his hand back towards the other two men. "Susan, these guys are your troops. You may know Roger."

Susan held her hand out to the gray, stoop-shouldered man. "Ah'm sorry for your loss, Mr. Kyber. Are you sure you want to do this?"

Roger shook her hand, solemn. "Thanks. I think your question is really if I'm not too old for it."

"Oh, well, no."

Amos said, "Roger is our driver. He's fría de hielo. He'll drive over or through anybody. He's also our sniper if we need one. My other friend here goes by the name of Tally. That's all you need to know."

She scrutinized the tall, muscular white man, dressed in leather with a do-rag on his long hair. "Tally?"

The white said, "Short for Taliban."

"Oh." There wasn't much to say after that.

Amos picked it up. "Here's the deal, guys. We have to play it loose when we get there. Only I give orders. Since we have Susan, we three hermanos go in, leave her with the motor running. The second car we'll plant close by in case something goes wrong with our exit. We don't kill nobody 'til I say, y yo prefiero que el cuchillo. The knife's your job Tally, so you take point. Let's saddle up, perros." The men grinned, moved quick. Young.

———

It all sounded simple but so much could go wrong. The chulos had a man outside the store with a minivan, loading three suitcases – they stole his keys to the front door after stealing his consciousness. Tally cinched him up with cable ties and duct tape and left him in his own back seat, ratcheted onto an arm rest. Susan waited in the get-away car. She heard a single barking sound from inside the store, a shot. Alarmed, she fidgeted in the front seat until her phone buzzed. It whispered up into her ear, "Come on in."

She crept forward through the empty merchandise displays, followed her way towards lights in the back. She found her three hombres in black masks, with two men on the floor in front of them, lying on their faces. One of the men groaned, a mumble of pain. Tally kicked him in the side of his head. "Shaddap!" She watched Tally practically dancing, holding in all that bottled-up energy.

Amos spoke sharp to him, in command. "Stay focused on the mission, Tally."

The second pimp lay unmoving, unconscious, a puddle of blood spread out from his knee. The pants were blown out in back; she could see the bone fragments, the ripped flesh.

Amos said, "Tape their eyes también. I don't want them seeing her."

Roger clutched keys in his hand – he scratched at the lock of a storeroom with them. "In here, Missy. If she's here." He wore a black military style rifle slung across his back. Susan scurried across the floor to his side – she glanced down and saw her own footprint, blocked out in blood.

Roger threw the door open and flipped on a light switch. He swept the room with his carbine, growled out, "We're here to save you. Para salvarlos, para salvarlos."

Susan crowded in beside him, shot a glance at Roger, a black balaclava over his head, the gun held at the ready. "Jeezus, Roger, you'll scare her!"

Inside three girls and a small boy, all brown, huddled up against the back wall in a corner. Two naked mattresses lay in the empty storeroom. The boy sniveled; snot hung under his nose. One of the girls wore only her underwear; the boy wore only a shirt.

"Which one of you is Juanita?" Susan asked. The oldest, a girl in pink, held her hand up, timid. "You're with me. Your text-er sent me. Do any of the rest of you speak English?"

"Sí," said one of the girls. "Quién es usted? Por favor, por favor no nos lastime más!"

Susan shook her head, not following. She pointed at the boy. "What's he here for?"

The three girls exchanged looks, the look. Juanita said, "The same."

Susan could feel the shock of the words, like a slap. "Christ! Are any of you related? Hermanos?"

"Sí," said the youngest girl, age ten perhaps. Her eyes shown round as the full moon, glimmering in tears. "She is my sister. He is my cousin. Está realmente aquí para ayudarnos? To get us away?"

Her sister whispered to her, huddled close with her arms around her.

"We're takin' you to the Family Advocacy Center. No one can hurt you there. Those men won't be able to get you back." She had the foursome up on their feet and dragged Juanita by the hand. Behind them Roger made shooing gestures, moving them along. From somewhere he had scooped up a pile of clothes – he held them to his chest with the plastic stock of his gun. All four children cried, bleating like sheep, tears running down their bowed faces and dripping off onto the floor.

Amos knelt by the head of one pimp, whispered in his ear. He had a knife in his hand, pointed down, and the point rotated, spun into the skin of the man's temple. He drilled a hole slow, slow into the man's head. Blood seeped down along the edge of the duct tape over the Latino's face.

As the children scurried by Amos jerked his head at Tally. "Cover them on the street. I got it here."

Susan parked Juanita in the front seat and shoved the other three children in the back. Roger lurched in behind the wheel and Susan took shotgun.

Tally thrust his head in the window, said, "Get the shit outa here. We'll take the backup car. I'm not done yet, and neither is Amos."

—⁓—

ROGER PARKED ACROSS THE STREET from the Center and they began the wait. Dawn came and light crawled across the hood. The trapped, stale air hung silent, as silent as fear in the car, and the hours till eight stretched out endless and jumpy. At least the three in the back seat slept for awhile. Leaning over the back of the seat, Susan touched the girl who spoke English on the knee. The girl's eyes leapt open and she gave a jump. "Oh. Muy malo. El peor – I wanted to die. Qué pasa ahora?"

"It's time now when this place opens up. When you get inside, there will be a policeman. Give him this piece of paper. It's the address where the bad men kept you. Tell him everything that happened."

The girl who spoke only Spanish burst into tears. "Qué pasa con la sangre de las partes?"

"What about my sister? She been bleeding for dos o tres días."

"Oh. They have nurses here too."

"Muchas gracias. La dulce Madre de Cristo. What happens to those men?"

Susan shook her head. "I don't know. But they can't get you here."

The girl shook her head, shared a glance with her sister. "Pero mi padre nos vendió."

"What?" The barbarity blew right past Susan. She frowned. "It's important we get away too, understand? You don't remember any-thing about us, do you?"

The girl nodded, her eyes flashed in the shadow of the back seat. "You wore las máscaras, sí?"

"Go then, and good luck." The three got out and rushed for the door. Susan and Roger watched them duck inside.

Susan said to the girl between them. "Juanita, time to talk, now the audience is gone." Roger turned the key. He drove away, headed up towards Central Avenue, the long way home.

"Yes." A tiny voice.

"That was so smart of you to hide your phone. Are you hurt?"

"There are sores where the ropes rubbed me. On my wrists." She held her hands out.

"Did they do anything to you? Did they have sex with you?"

"Rape me?"

"Yeah."

"They were saving me for a big customer. One who likes vírgenes. Two of the chulos used the mojadas, and one liked the little boy. They only made me watch. And ... you know ... spattered it on me."

Susan said, "You poor baby! Why did they keep you there, in the music store?"

"They said they needed to break us in."

"Did your mother sell you to those pimps?"

"Yes." She gazed down at her knees, black hair falling into her face.

"So, you're pretty much done at home, huh?"

"I can't go back if she's there."

Roger said, "That's got to be the truest thing I've heard." He turned north on the Interstate.

Susan asked, "How about you stay with me, hide out at my place?"

Juanita, eyes wide, said, "Okay."

"Just till we decide what's what. We'll take it a day at a time." Juanita broke into sobs, little grizzling exhalations, and Susan clasped her up in her arms.

Roger awkwardly patted the girl on the head. "It's going to be okay. You're smart and strong. My mother would have liked you."

THREE STRONG COFFEES EXHALED STEAM in front of the men. They leaned close, since Julio's breakfast rush swirled around them. Roger asked, "Did you kill 'em?"

"No."

"I would gladly have killed them."

Tally said, "I wanted to torch the place, with them inside. Amos wouldn't let me."

Amos said, "Dangerous. Cops, forensics, snitches. Criminal use of a gun, that's enough."

Roger swung his head around at Amos, took aim. "You weren't in the car with the kids."

Tally asked, "Where are they, the kids?"

"Susan has Juanita and the other three are hidden away in the Albuquerque Family Center."

Amos said, "That's good then."

Tally asked, "Isn't Susan, you know, a dyke?"

Amos snorted. "You think she's gonna force a fourteen-year-old? Change her over to una lesbiana? Grow up, chico."

"What I wanna know, Amos," asked Roger. "What were you talking about with that chulo back in that store?"

"The pandillero? I got a name. Who he works for."

"Handy."

"I was pissing out our territory. I gave him a message to take back."

Roger asked, "What message?"

"They come to our tierra nativa again, we will bring the war to them."

"Yeah!" said Tally, a dreamy look in his eyes.

CHAPTER THIRTY-ONE

HELEN PARCH SNIFFED IN THE dryness, the particular odor of paper and glue that had lost all hint of moisture years ago. Books surrounded her, aromatic husks of lives scribbled, printed and confined to shelves. Against the old metal-framed windows in the library wall, an angry fly buzzed, battering itself against the glass, and sought escape into the fall afternoon. She considered the fly and squinted at the strong backlight, the Albuquerque sunshine that arrowed through the windows and showed the dust motes floating in the air above the empty tables.

She stalked out from behind the front desk, silent in white orthopedic shoes below her powder blue skirt. She leaned over GMR's shoulder and laid a yellow legal tablet on the table in front of him, sliding aside his picture book. "You need this."

He gazed up into her face, silent.

"It took me a good long while to clean up the fly-leaf in that book, the one where you drew all those sketches. I made a xerox, before I began erasing. You can keep it here in the library." She laid the copy on top of the yellow paper.

He stretched up his brown hand, touching the copy.

"We'll set you up a file folder. Come with me – bring your paper."

Her hand dropped onto the back of his neck, as if she might pinch it in a vise of dry-skinned fingers.

She marched him to the front desk and around to the interior. Tugging out a drawer in her file cabinet she got an empty manila folder, and snatching the xerox from his fingers, filed it. On the label tag, Helen wrote GMR. "We'll keep the folder in back, here. You can come and use it anytime. I have pencils in this drawer." She drew out the drawer above the kneehole. A new box of art pencils, in a gleaming plastic box. "I have an eraser also." One of the good gum erasers.

Solemn, GMR picked up the box. "Thank you." He flashed out a grin. "This is cool!"

Helen smiled back – she had finally pleased him. "Let's find you a place to draw." She steered him out from behind the front desk. "You should use this table here, near where I work. Now, come along." She sailed across the library. The boy trailed in her wake. "You haven't seen these yet. We have more than Art books, we have books on *how* to make art." In amongst the stacks, they sank cross-legged to the floor and viewed books on the bottom two shelves. She glanced down to see her panty-hosed knee pressed up against his grubby hip, her skirt in folds and his tattered shorts in a dusty innocence. "See? We'll choose one. Place this slip of paper in where you pulled out the book. You'll bring the book back here, later. Now, to work."

Back at his station, GMR hunched up to the table, pencil in his left hand. The book lay open at the top of his pad. The yellow paper already showed smudges under the edge of his palm. The pencil dug deep into the pad, making lines short and severe, lacking the flow of practice. He recreated the face of a tiger, with the cat eyes prominent and too large. She rested beside him, not too close, a hand lying on his far collarbone, cradling his shoulders with her arm. She could feel his body heat. The Library rested quiet, sleeping in during a Saturday afternoon.

—*m*—

IN THE COOL OF A Monday evening, Harry tugged open the door of Julio's Taquería and swung his eyes across the room. GMR worked at a table near the cash register, with paper napkins and flatware spread out before him. Groaning, Harry settled himself into the chair beside the boy, so he faced the front of the restaurant.

The boy picked up one spoon, one fork, one knife, held them in his left hand, and tucked a corner of a napkin under his thumb. Twisting his left hand, he wound the napkin around the utensils. On the table lay a slick roll gridded with small paper circles; GMR peeled one off and stuck it on the corner of the napkin, then placed the cutlery on a stack of bundles, a log pile of paper and aluminum.

Harry said, "I thought you were a sous-chef."

"We did all that for the day."

"Do you have a lot of these to do?"

GMR shrugged his shoulders up, dropped them. He picked up a spoon. "Not many. Most of what we serve is hand food. People don't use forks."

"I suppose that's true."

"Everyone likes the green chili stew. Stew needs spoons."

"Do you make the stew?"

"I do the chilis. They come off the grill all black and burned. I rub off the skin, then I push the seeds out. Then I cut it up with a knife." He made the rocking motion of a knife dicing.

"Sounds complicated."

"It's better if you don't touch your eyes. That stings." He placed another bundle on the pile.

Harry asked, "Do you like watches?"

"Dunno."

"I like watches. I got you one. See, it's got a cloth band that uses Velcro to fasten. The time is shown on this screen here." He shoved the watch towards the boy.

GMR took it, held the watch like it might bite. "Are you sure?"

"Richard sold it to me. Mr. Martin. Here, let me adjust it, for the first time." Harry gripped the boy's hand and wrapped the watch around his wrist. They both gazed at the watch, wound around a boy's arm held in a man's hand. Harry released GMR and leaned back. "There."

The boy rotated his wrist, gazing at all views of the watch. "Thanks." His white teeth shown out in a grin.

Harry said, "You know, you remind me of someone."

The boy asked, "Why are you so sad?"

CHAPTER THIRTY-TWO

"WE NEED A FAVOR, SOULFUL." Susan parked herself on the edge of the desk.

"Small talk over, Susan? If it's a bail bond, I don't think so. Both of you strike me as flight risks, and margins are pitiful this month. Especially after the ads you bought with my money." He swept his mass of blonde hair back with his hand and smiled to himself.

Lavinia rolled her chair towards him, sending it creeping across the linoleum. "We didn't buy them. Your association AABBA bought them. But that's not the favor we came for."

"Really?"

Susan traced a mysterious outline on the desktop with her finger, watching as she mapped it out. "It's occurred to us that you know – ah – criminals."

"Please don't tell my mother. She thinks so well of her fair-haired boy."

Susan wrinkled up her eyebrows, leaned forward. "Seriously. Criminals have talents that the rest of us don't."

"That is right. I've noticed that very thing. But they are seldom rewarded for using those talents."

Lavinia said, "Fortunately for you – it provides your living. But we wondered if you could talk to someone with a particular talent."

Susan drawled out, "We need new identities. For Juanita and for GMR."

"Really? Well. I have a couple of clients that do ID. I might be able to get you a discount."

Lavinia asked, "How does it work?"

"Births aren't tied together with deaths in New Mexico registers. My – clients – pick out someone the right age, sex and ethnicity who died and then go back and reuse the birth. Voila, instant identity."

"What will we need?" Susan asked.

"For kids their ages, all you want is a birth certificate and maybe a social security number. You can get fake school transcripts, but why pay for the complication?"

"Because we might want them accepted in a new school. Can you get forged adoption papers?"

"Oo. Not heard of that one. Have to ask."

"Would you?"

"Oh, sure. I'll send out some feelers this afternoon."

Lavinia said, "Well, this is criminal, but it's still ethical. We just get in deeper and deeper with this boy, don't we?"

Susan laughed, her voice pealing out. "Yeah, wild, ain't it?"

Lavinia slapped her hands on the desk. "Well, I'm glad that's settled. I've got to go. It's nearly time for Tenn's lunch."

Susan said, "Soulful, why don't you let me buy you lunch at the Taquería? Consider it a down payment."

"Okay, sure. But I bet it costs me later." Out on the sidewalk, he nodded at a police cruiser going by. "Ever notice how cop cars change the feel in a neighborhood? And why is it my friends are always the nervous ones?"

Lavinia frowned, watching the squad car prowl its way down the strip, creeping along. "I wonder what trouble they're after?"

The cops had just found trouble, but it had happened already, yesterday afternoon. Where and who were things of the past. Now it would be all about what-next.

———

THE "WHO" HAD BEEN INTIENDA. She drove up to the house, still in her old junker of a car. She'd never have a way to buy that new one, not with the way the money evaporated. And not with Whit in Arkansas stealing cheap American sedans. She patted the scruffy, bruised purse on the seat beside her. At least this week it had bulged with money long enough to pay for Amy's enrollment.

Sauntering down the side of the house and around, she yanked open the back screen door. Stopped.

Bud waited at the table. Over the last year her son had changed from a child to a man. The fist tattoo had been joined by a chain that circled his neck, ornamented with red spikes. His brown hair hung in a shock over his face, a counterpoint to the buzz on the sides.

"Home for a change?" she asked her son.

"You did it, didn't you?"

"What?"

"Don't play dumb, Mom."

"I don't know what you're talking about." She made her voice as hard and unyielding as she knew how.

"Word is, you're broke. And you got Amy in that special school. An expensive one."

"We're having trouble making ends meet."

"Yeah, yeah, yeah. All of Dad's money is going up your nose."

"I don't know what you're talking about," she repeated, louder.

212

He let the silence lay between them for a minute. She still poised in the door. "So, where is Juanita? Where is mi hermana?"

"In school."

"Really? I was talking to Uvaldo. He's got an uncle that works southwest 'Querque.'

"Your hoodie friends," she sneered.

"They'd never do what you done." His face scowled, his lip drawn back.

"What is that?" She clomped across the kitchen, her feet loud on the linoleum.

"It's not bad enough you ruined Amy with your drinking. You sold Juanita to a pimp. He's moving her down to Cruces; he's gonna work her at the airbase."

"That's not true." She snatched up a glass and the Mexican brandy off the counter, turned around to face him. Something in her hands. Her shaking hands.

"You didn't have to love her. You were just supposed to take care of her. Es el código, you bitch."

"Watch your mouth!"

He got up, both hands on the table. He glowered at her. "You are the worst goddamn mother in the world. You wrote us off years ago, and you just been goin' through the motions."

"You stupid niñito. What the hell do you know about it!"

He advanced around the table, and she sidled the other way. "I know a lot. I know what a worthless piece of trash you are."

"I'm worthless? You'll never even understand what it means to be a man like your father. You're just going to sink into that gang life where they decide everything for you. That is, until you end up dead on the street."

He stalked around the table, she backed away, circling. "The gang is a better place than here, a better family than you'll ever give me. You're such a cunt, Mother."

"You little bastard! How dare you call me that?" She threw the bottle of brandy at him. It sailed past his head, crashed into the breadbox on top of the refrigerator.

He froze. His scowl disappeared. He laughed, the sound ringing throughout the kitchen. "You know what happens in the gang when someone betrays us? Sells us out?"

"What?" She heard her voice crack in anger.

"We finish it." He jerked the pistol out from the waistband behind his back, out from under his T-shirt.

She jeered, "You aren't going to use that."

"I hadn't made up my mind. Until right now. Mother." He held the gun straight out, three feet from her chest. He squeezed and the round slammed in between her fleshy breasts, knocking her back into the kitchen cabinets. She folded her hands around the bullet hole. She couldn't hear – except the ringing in her head. An ooze of blood between her fingers. She drew in a breath, a rattle. Head tilted down, a statue of a praying saint. She had forgotten how to pray. Bud held the gun out towards her, sideways like the bangers on TV. He shot her again. Another seven times. Slow, correcting for recoil each time. All the way down to the floor.

THE FIRST COPS ON THE scene had stretched yellow tape across the front door. Impotent, it sagged as droopy and used up as the house itself. The police pathologist had parked his van in the drive behind Intienda's car. He knelt in the kitchen, beside the body. Two uniforms leaned against the walls, with nothing better to do than watch. The forensic assistant hunched over in a chair across the room, texting on his phone.

A cigarette hung out of the pathologist's mouth and dropped ash into the crime scene. He trickled burnt tobacco smoke out of his mouth, mixing it with the cloying smell of the blood coating the floor. "She took maybe six, maybe seven rounds. It's hard to be sure with all the tears in the clothes. The one in the face though, I think we can count that one as guaranteeing death."

A plainclothes policeman crouched beside him. "How long?"

"Body's cold. Twelve hours or more. We'll be able to do a proper look and get a liver temp when I have her logged in and naked in the drawer."

The detective said, "We got eight shells from a nine millimeter scattered around. Beats me how somebody can burn through a mag and no one reports it for hours. It's not like you can't hear a frickin' nine a block away."

The pathologist hemmed. "Perhaps the local denizens are somewhat shy of the police."

A cop leaning up against the counter snorted. "Ya think?"

The ranking policeman said, "We'll soon know all about that too. I got people out canvassing the neighborhood. That's the least of my worries, though."

"Oh? Other complications?"

"Husband is a habitual criminal, wanted right now for grand theft auto. His jacket doesn't indicate he'd do this, but you never know. And ...."

"And what?" The doctor zipped the body into the bag for transport, a long ripping sound that stopped the background conversation. His assistant lurched to his feet and shuffled forward, rolling up the gurney.

Shaking his head, the cop said, "There's four goddamn missing kids."

"Family. Always messy." The doctor grunted as he got up and dusted his hands. "See you tomorrow at the morgue." He waved a hand at his assistant, urging him to get on with it.

———

CLEANING ON HER KNEES, ILENE McKennet heard the tinkling bell on the front door of the store. A policeman in uniform entered Key to the Kingdom, notebook in hand. Bemused, he stopped and gazed around the religious store and past to the back wall, where the locksmith tools and grinders waited. He chuckled, rubbing the buzz cut on his head.

As he strode forward, his gaze locked on Ilene. She stopped dusting the racks at the ends of the aisles, where the Jesus key chains and other sundry items hung, and struggled off her knees to her feet.

"Nice place you got here," said the policeman. His childish head, his smooth unlined face stuck out of a black collar and tie too large for him.

"Why thank you, Officer."

"Course, I mostly see the insides of bars, or where your average domestic disturbance occurs. Nice to be someplace where there's no blood or alcohol."

A smell of burning tar wafted across the room to her. She threw a quick glimpse over her shoulder. The Devil, perched on Donnie's stool by the grinding machine, snorted. "No reason a holy-roller store won't end up a crime scene too," he said.

She frowned and twitched at the Devil. He snickered and mimicked her scowl. She faced away from him, towards the boy in uniform, and asked, "Can I help you with anything?"

"We're pursuing enquiries in the neighborhood. I wonder if you saw or heard anything yesterday afternoon."

"Heard anything?"

"Out of the ordinary."

"Oh, I wasn't here then. I would have been at home. We live over on 12th and Aztec in a nice apartment complex. If you don't mind me asking, what is this about?"

"Ongoing investigation, so I can't say much. Someone reported a shooting a block over. We're also searching for five people. I have pictures of three."

She shuffled the two steps to her check-out stand. At the register, she clicked on a gooseneck lamp. "Now, Officer, what do you have?"

The policeman said, "We're looking for this man." He snapped down a photo of Whit Whittington in the circle of light.

"Yes, he looks familiar. He's never been in while I was here, but I would think he's part of the neighborhood. Handsome man, in a pretty-boy way." Her finger tapped Whit's forehead. "Try Rip's. That's where so many of our sinners can be found. May God lead them back into righteousness." The Devil sniggered, back there in the dimness.

"I'm also on the lookout for four children from this family. Their names are Amy, Gerald, Juanita and William Whittington. The two boys may go by Gerry and Bud." She shook her head, doubtful. He said, "I have a photo of Juanita."

"Oh, yes, I know her. She has her hair cut here at Mr. Russell's. Difficult child. You know how they can get."

"No, I don't quite know what you mean."

"They drop into a bad mood at that age and don't come out for years."

217

He nodded. "The beauty shop, huh. Have you seen her around lately?"

"No, not for weeks."

The policeman placed a copy of a school picture on the counter. "I also have a picture of Gerry. Have you seen this boy around?"

A rooster crowed in the store. She whipped her head around – the Devil reared his head back and extended his neck; the loose skin below his chin shook back and forth. Her eyes jumped from policeman to the Devil and back to the policeman. "Did you hear that?"

"Hear what?" The policeman shrugged. "Naah, quiet in here. The photo, ma'am?"

Distinct, low, growling, the Devil said, "Here it is, the big chance. Redemption or damnation, pleasure or sterile virtue – your choice. What's an old biddy to do, deny me three times?" He hopped down from the stool and cantered forward.

Surely, the policeman would hear, would sense his presence, smell the evil! Eyes wide, she stared at the cop – his face hung over her, relaxed and vacant.

She stared at the photo. "He looks like he's about eight."

"Ten, actually," said the policeman.

The Devil scratched her neck with his fingernail, laid his hand on the photo. She stared down at his jaundiced skin, the broken and gnawed fingernails, red gunk caked under them. The Devil whispered in her ear. "Come, come, Ilene. Let's finish what we began, you and I. Join the conspiracy and hide the boy. If you do, I'll give you Cheezsy, full time. Just one tiny white lie." He cackled, breathed out that smell of turpentine, wafted it across her face – his gift.

She sucked in her breath. She huffed it out. "Oh yes, that's the boy. They call him GMR. He lives in the apartment above Rip's.

A ten-year-old boy, all by himself. I ask you, is that right?" Tears sprang into her eyes. "It's time for Deliverance."

"Ma'am?"

"I mean, we could ... you ought ... it's your job. Go and get him."

—•••—

Lavinia glared out through the screen door, ignoring the plain-clothes detective beside her. He had bad posture and a cheap suit.

Her seventy-odd years rode her face and her upper lip had the deep vertical wrinkles of age and disapproval. She pursed up her mouth around that persimmon taste of anger. Behind her the bar rattled on with its evening business, while in the alley, Albuquerque shredded up another life.

Under the halo of Rip's small backdoor light, an official New Mexico CYFD car with the two front doors open filled the alley. Out there Richard Martin conferred with a man and a woman in business dress. Lavinia could hear Richard's voice, raised a bit, "No, we didn't take him in. He just hung around, you know. It *still* was better than what he had with his family." The woman confronting him said something Lavinia couldn't hear. Richard responded, "Because we know all about that family." The man and the woman faced off against Richard. Richard added, loud as a bull, "Believe me, I've got more experience with runaways than you do. Christ on a crutch."

Lavinia rang her voice out clear and hard. "Leave it, Richard. You're going to make it worse." He shot a glance over his shoulder, but didn't continue. Instead, he thrust his head through the car window into the back seat. Lavinia could just make out GMR in there, a small spot of darkness in a dark alley. She watched GMR's head drop. He seemed diminutive beside the woman who shared the seat with him.

The detective beside Lavinia murmured. She answered the question he repeated from a moment ago. "No, I don't know anything about what happened to Intienda Whittington. I just know what the boy told me months ago."

"And what did he tell you?"

"He told me he was never going back."

"So all of you took on this runaway and hid him from the authorities?"

"First of all, I did it. No one else. And second, I didn't hide him from the authorities, only his family."

"Failure to report." He wrote in his notebook.

She snorted. "Yes, I confess Failure to Report. Is there a law?"

"Maybe. I work homicide – you'll have to ask the Kiddie Cops over there." He gestured to the officers in the alley with his pen.

"Thank you. I will." Lavinia stepped through the door and allowed the screen to slam in the face of the detective. She approached the two standing by the car. "Hello. I'm Lavinia Dortmund. I'm the one who has been helping the boy, who gave him a place to live. What happens to him now?"

The two glanced at each other. She could see they were weighing up whether they would respond at all. Turf established, civilian diminished, the man eked out some explanation. "Family's out. Got a dad who's a person of interest in a felony. Got a mother lying dead in the morgue."

"So then?"

He decided to give the rest of the story. "Court order and foster care, I would think. We'll keep him at the Center until the Court sorts it out."

Lavinia asked, "Is there any way I can be involved with the boy, stay in touch, visit?"

Acid etched the woman cop's words, "I think it's time you leave it to the professionals. You amateurs screwed this one up already." Lavinia lowered her eyes.

Voice warmer, the man said, "Later, maybe. If the Department makes a favorable evaluation and the foster family decides yes. You have a chance for visitation."

CHAPTER THIRTY-THREE

G MR's HOUSE HAD DISAPPEARED, ALONG with a half dozen blocks of trailers, bungalows and casitas. Gone were the little houses that had defined a neighborhood proud in the '50s impoverished in the '80s, broke in the '90s and collapsed into a mixed-race ghetto. No mixing now. Six blocks stretched from here to the River ranchos and depicted a bull-dozed jumble of rubble, a desert of tracks cut by massive equipment, punctuated by toppled trees and holes. Of course they had left the riverside horse farms alone, the big houses protected by their white fences and green grass. NMDOT had cut the narrowest possible track across one ranchito to the River.

Nonsensical piles, heaped up here and scraped down there, painted a wasteland. Tenn searched for a pattern. His head hurt.

A snapped-off telephone pole leaned over by the back door of Rip's. Tenn thought about the pole. He could get a better view up there. Once at the top, he could just give up to the splintered stake – wrap his arms around it and slide down the splinters until they consumed him. The physical pain would be so much better.

Behind him in Rip's, everything worth taking had been stripped out. He could barely stand to look at it. The bar had disappeared and the coolers had been trucked off. His abandoned walkway ran across the back like a miniature stage. The scratched metal shelves for the package liquor section still divided the space, dented and worn, but the wiring for the neon hung naked out of the wall. He had left two tables that were past their time and a broken chair he had used as a step stool. His shoes lay in the middle of the floor, in the light of the open front door. One was tipped over; the other still had the laces tied. Socks were missing.

Barefoot, he slumped on the step and contemplated starting his life over. He poured a slug past his lips into his mouth from the bourbon bottle in his hand, and felt the light of God burn down his throat – the flush of wellness that ran through his body like an orgasm.

BOB THE TAXIDERMIST HEFTED BACK the sledge hammer and beat at the wall. The cabinet had already fallen to the floor, a heap of pressboard splinters. It wasn't enough.

He had thought, as he swung the sledge over and over, he would wear his anger down to a panting sixty-year old wheeze. But to his surprise, he was able to continue on and on. In the midst of the deep crunch of each blow and his litany of swearing, the front door banged open. Mr. Russell charged in, into a disheveled space of broken cabinets and heaped-up animal heads.

Mr. Russell, distracted by the paleolithic mound of animal heads – some of whom stared glass-eyed at him – didn't say anything at first. Bob glanced over his shoulder, and dismissing the hair stylist, continued his assault on their common wall. The cinderblock had crumbled far enough to create a torso-sized hole on Bob's side.

Mr. Russell said, "Dobbel! What the hell are you doing?" He threw his hands onto his hips, stood as tall as he could.

Bob threw the sledge down at the base of the wall and wheeled about. "What the hell are *you* doing? They condemned your shop. They're going to tear it down come Monday. And you're in there cutting hair like it's just another day."

Russell, dressed in his blue smock and holding a toothed pair of scissors, gaped at Bob. With a gasp, he spit out, "I have customers."

"Holy Jesus! A day and a half away and you got customers. They're going to find you half-moved out."

"I'm not moving. And I'd appreciate it if you'd leave my wall alone."

"Not moving? Are you crazy?"

Russell gazed around at the destruction in the Taxidermy shop. "Am *I* crazy? Look what you've done here!"

"Not enough, believe you me. I'm finished, and nobody gets anything out of this, least of all them."

"So you're not leaving either?"

"Of course I am, you idiot. I'm going to Florida where my daughter lives. And what are you gonna do when they come on Monday?"

"I have some loyal customers. We'll continue doing what we've always done. Until they arrest me." He fluttered his hand like a bird on the wing, distressed.

"Goddamn it to hell Russell. Don't you think it's a little late to choose sides? Where were you when we needed you? Stinking little haircutter." His voice trailed off. "Too late, goddamn it."

Russell said, quiet and meek, "Maybe too late, but I finally got to the party. Now, if you don't mind, please don't raise any more dust in the Cut 'N Curl."

———

Strange. Santa Fe was just – Santa Fe. Juanita had no other way to describe it, not in the Bosque words she knew. The table in front of her held her course work, the little room held the table, the little stucco held the room, and the crooked street lined with piñon and chamisa held the little house. For dinner they would have vegetarian tamales and posole Susan picked up on the way home from work. Then in the cold of the evening, they would drive down to the Plaza and stroll among the luminarias and gaze into the shop windows, peering into a foreign world.

She stretched, extending the muscles in her neck left and right, then turned back to her homework. Mary Beth, passing in the hallway, said, "Sit up straight, dear."

"Yes ma'am."

Mary Beth paused. Juanita liked the way she dressed, in a blouse that mimicked Mexican peasant clothes, a wrap-around skirt of many colors, a giant concha belt. It was kind of sexy, for an old lady. "You wanted to ask something?"

Juanita obliged. "I need a theme for my essay. So, the Greeks were pretty much perfect for their time? I mean, they invented democracy, right?"

"Dig deeper, Chloe. They did practice a pure form of democracy in Athens, but it was only for men of position. Sparta, right next door, perfected the military state. And all Greek cities suppressed women and promoted slavery."

Chloe. Juanita couldn't get used to her new name. "Oh. What does all that mean?"

"So, maybe your essay should be about first steps to democracy, or how they were a complex civilization trying many different things."

"Okay. I'll think about it." She knew what the essay would be. It would be what she could con Susan and her partner Mary Beth into telling her. Why should anyone mess around with Greek democracy? It had nothing to do with life, with her life past and present.

225

Until she turned eighteen, she would be their Chloe, and after that, she'd see. Maybe she'd change back to Juanita, but in the meantime, she had the sweet life. She thanked God her mother was dead. The one good thing Bud ever did.

—~~—

RICHARD HUNKERED UP ON A stool amidst a sea of boxes in a new storefront, five blocks away from the abandoned pawnshop. Julio and Amos, collapsed on the floor across the room, lazy and languid. They grumbled Spanish phrases back and forth between them. First Julio sighed. "Estoy cansado. Estoy hecho. Terminado."

"Ninguna chite," Amos said.

"What? What did you say?" Richard asked.

Amos waved his hand, like a big bird that couldn't quite get off the ground. "He just say he's whipped. He don't think he can do this no more. As for me, I'm sweating like a fat man, a real gordo."

Richard grinned to think Amos thought *he* was fat. "We may not be able to open for business soon, but we got both the Taquería and the Pawnshop moved. It's a miracle. The poet said,

> As he drew near, he gazed upon the door
> Ne'er to be enter'd more by him or Sin.
> He clattered his keys at a a great rate,
> and sweated through his apostolic skin:
> Of course his perspiration was but ichor,
> Or some such other spiritual liquor.

That's Keats, one of his drinking songs, I think. Or *Ephemeron*."

"Chu say so, bro." Julio sighed. "What I wouldn't give for a beer."

"Wait." Richard surged to his feet and stomped into the back room. He returned with a chilled blue bottle of vodka, dripping with condensation. "Here." Grunting, he bent over and offered the bottle to Julio.

Julio said, "That's pretty good stuff, Richard. You sure you want to share it out with acabados?"

"You moved that pawned Coke machine for me. Have a swig."

Julio unscrewed the cap, swallowed a mouthful and coughed hard. "Cristo, that's smooth." He glanced over at his brother. "I'd pass you this, hermano, but that would be a bad idea, seeing you an alcohólico en recuperación. Besides, this too good for you. Here you go, Richard." He attempted to hand the bottle back, holding it out at arm's length.

"Naah. I think I'll wait."

"Wait for what?"

"It will still be there tomorrow."

Amos asked, "Chu sober, Richard?"

"Regrettably. Is it true that it can be habit forming?"

―――

HARRY THOUGHT ABOUT MOVING BACK to the old neighborhood. He thought about it a lot. His nook of an office off Central was okay, but way too expensive. He had a bar nearby, but the people in the bar dressed in a hipster way he couldn't quite fathom. Even his father's watch felt out of place and had stopped running.

A bank statement lay in front of him, red-flagged with his overdrafts. He knew he had to get the expenses under control, but this was the wrong neighborhood for that. The psychic fog he inhabited was gray and rising, now above his head. He slumped, unmoving. The sunlight coming in the window lengthened, crawled up the wall towards dusk. He didn't see the deep amber at all, only the disjoint, gray images inside his head.

His phone rang and he pushed it to voice mail. "Hi, Dad, it's Miriam. Pick up. I know you're there."

Stung by the accusation, he pressed the button. "Hello, baby. How are you."

"I'm great. California's great. The job's great. It's you we should worry about."

"Why worry about me?"

"Da-ad. You've been moping around ever since that bar of yours died. It's just not natural."

"Who says I'm moping around?"

"I do. Mom agrees. If you want, I can put her on the phone and she'll tell you herself."

"God forbid. Then I could get really depressed."

"So why don't you move out here, to be close to me?" She got right to it, like always.

"Baby, if I can't afford Albuquerque, what makes you think I can afford San Diego?"

"Take up something new. Make big bucks."

What he couldn't say to her was "The grave is here, in Albuquerque." Instead he said, "I like my life here." His voice sounded thin to himself.

"Yeah, right." Much like her mother. Judgmental from an early age. "Dad, are you there?"

"I was thinking this afternoon. About your brother Eddie. Do you ever think about him?"

"I was pretty young when he died, Dad. I sometimes think I remember him and I sometimes think I'm remembering what you've told me. See what I mean?"

"Yeah. He was ten, you were six."

"Six and a half."

"Six and a half," he agreed. She had always been a half ahead of him.

FALL 2010

CHAPTER THIRTY-FOUR

RECEPTION DIRECTED LAVINIA AND HELEN from the seating area, past the rope and back to the desk in its cubicle. Lavinia gawked, milking the visit, the first and last time she would ever be here. Behind the metal desk a very large black woman was ensconced behind mounds of paper. She had punctuated her cubicle wall with pictures of her children and little jokey signs that had been given to her or that she had bought. A helium balloon now sagged down past a bookshelf, drooping onto a stuffed blue hippopotamus. The woman raised her reading glasses up on her large coffee colored forehead. "Miss Parch. It's been awhile. Thanks for coming in."

"Mrs. Bronson." Helen shook the offered hand. "This is my friend, Lavinia Dortmund. She came along for moral support."

"Welcome, Mizz Dortmund. Have a seat, you two." The two women milled around in front of the plastic chairs and sank into concave discomfort. Lavinia leaned back, Helen perched on the edge. "Paper work is back at last, Miss Parch."

"Well, you did say I should expect a six week wait."

"Six weeks *after* the father signed away his rights."

"But in the meantime, your staff did come out for the home visit and I've seen a couple of e-mails."

"I've reviewed everything and we've been to committee. I'm pleased to let you know that New Mexico Children Youth and Families Department has approved your request for adoption. You'll have to appear in court, but Gerald effectively is one of your family now."

Lavinia reached across and patted Helen's hand. Helen relaxed. "Oh thank God."

"Now there are several places where you have to sign and I've tagged those. While you're doing that, I need to go consult with a colleague. I'll be right back." Mrs. Bronson handed over a clutch of paper, got up, and with short steps clumped away. Her thighs made swishing sounds.

Helen breathed out in a whoosh and picked up a cheap ballpoint off the desk. "Last chance to turn back, I suppose." She smiled her thin smile, her black hair seized back in a severe bun.

Lavinia asked, "No second thoughts, Helen?"

"You can trust me." She began signing.

About the Author

Scott Archer Jones is currently living and working on his sixth novel in northern New Mexico, after stints in the Netherlands, Scotland and Norway plus less exotic locations. He's worked for a power company, grocers, a lumberyard, an energy company (for a very long time), and a winery. He has launched three books. Jupiter and Gilgamesh, a Novel of Sumeria and Texas in 2014, The Big Wheel in 2015, and this one, *a rising tide of people swept away*.

https://www.facebook.com/ScottArcherJones
www.scottarcherjones.com

Fomite

A fomite is a medium capable of transmitting infectious organisms from one individual to another.

"The activity of art is based on the capacity of people to be infected by the feelings of others." Tolstoy, *What Is Art?*

Writing a review on Amazon, Good Reads, Shelfari, Library Thing or other social media sites for readers will help the progress of independent publishing. To submit a review, go to the book page on any of the sites and follow the links for reviews. Books from independent presses rely on reader to reader communications.

For more information or to order any of our books, visit
http://www.fomitepress.com/FOMITE/Our_Books.html

Nothing Beside Remains
Jaysinh Birjépatil

The Way None
of This Happened
Mike Breiner

Summer on the
Cold War Planet
Paula Closson Buck

Foreign Tales of
Exemplum and Woe
J. C. Ellefson

Free Fall/Caída libre
Tina Escaja

Speckled Vanities
Marc Estrin

Fomite

Off to the Next Wherever
John Michael Flynn

Derail This Train Wreck
Daniel Forbes

Semitones
Derek Furr

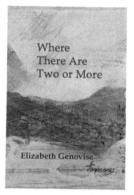

Where There Are Two or More
Elizabeth Genovise

In A Family Way
Zeke Jarvis

A Free, Unsullied Land
Maggie Kast

Shadowboxing With Bukowski
Darrell Kastin

Feminist on Fire
Coleen Kearon

Thicker Than Blood
Jan English Leary

Fomite

*A Guide
to the Western Slopes*
Roger Lebovitz

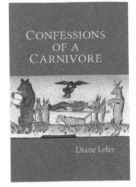

Confessions of a Carnivore
Diane Lefer

*Unborn Children of
America*
Michele Markarian

Shirtwaist Story
Delia Bell Robinson

Isles of the Blind
Robert Rosenberg

What We Do For Love
Ron Savage

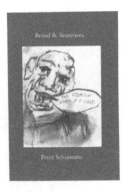

Bread & Sentences
Peter Schumann

*Planet Kasper
Voume 2*
Peter Schumann

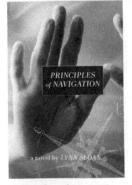

Principles of Navigation
Lynn Sloan

Fomite

Industrial Oz
Scott T. Starbuck

Among Angelic Orders
Susan Thoma

*The Inconveniece
of the Wings*
Silas Dent Zobal

Fomite

More Titles from Fomite...

Joshua Amses — *Raven or Crow*

Joshua Amses — *The Moment Before an Injury*

Jaysinh Birjepatel — *The Good Muslim of Jackson Heights*

Antonello Borra — *Alfabestiario*

Antonello Borra — *AlphaBetaBestiaro*

Jay Boyer — *Flight*

David Brizer — *Victor Rand*

David Cavanagh — *Cycling in Plato's Cave*

Dan Chodorkoff — *Loisada*

Michael Cocchiarale — *Still Time*

James Connolly — *Picking Up the Bodies*

Greg Delanty — *Loosestrife*

Catherine Zobal Dent — *Unfinished Stories of Girls*

Mason Drukman — *Drawing on Life*

Zdravka Evtimova —*Carts and other stories*

Zdravka Evtimova — *Sinfonia Bulgarica*

Anna Faktorovich — *Improvisational Arguments*

Derek Furr — *Suite for Three Voices*

Stephen Goldberg — *Screwed and other plays*

Barry Goldensohn — *The Hundred Yard Dash Man*

Barry Goldensohn — *The Listener Aspires to the Condition of Music*

R. L. Green — *When You Remember Deir Yassin*

Greg Guma — *Dons of Time*

Andrei Guriuanu — *Body of Work*

Fomite

Ron Jacobs — *All the Sinners Saints*

Ron Jacobs — *Short Order Frame Up*

Ron Jacobs — *The Co-conspirator's Tale*

Kate MaGill — *Roadworthy Creature, Roadworthy Craft*

Tony Magistrale — *Entanglements*

Gary Miller — *Museum of the Americas*

Ilan Mochari — *Zinsky the Obscure*

Jennifer Anne Moses — *Visiting Hours*

Sherry Olson —*Four-Way Stop*

Andy Potok — *My Father's Keeper*

Janice Miller Potter — *Meanwell*

Jack Pulaski — *Love's Labours*

Charles Rafferty — *Saturday Night at Magellan's*

Joseph D. Reich — *The Hole That Runs Through Utopia*

Joseph D. Reich — *The Housing Market*

Joseph D. Reich — *The Derivation of Cowboys and Indians*

Kathryn Roberts — *Companion Plants*

David Schein — *My Murder and other local news*

Peter Schumann — *Planet Kasper, Volume Two*

Fred Skolnik — *Rafi's Tale*

Lynn Sloan — *Principles of Navigation*

L.E. Smith — *The Consequence of Gesture*

L.E. Smith — *Views Cost Extra*

L.E. Smith — *Travers' Inferno*

Susan Thomas — *The Empty Notebook Interrogates Itself*

Fomite

CPSIA information can be obtained
at www.ICGtesting.com
Printed in the USA
LVHW091538280519
619299LV00005B/921/P

9 781942 515432